THE GIORDANO MAFIA PREQUEL

THE GIRL WITHOUT HANDS

AWARD WINNING AUTHOR

INDIA R. ADAMS

THE GIORDANO MAFIA

THE GIORDANO MAFIA PREQUEL

THE GIRL WITHOUT HANDS

AWARD WINNING AUTHOR

INDIA R. ADAMS

SERIOUS AUTHOR WARNING

(The original release of The Girl Without Hands was in the … Anthology.)

When I was invited to this project by Dani, I was so excited because my mother had a children's theater and loved all children's stories, such as Grimm Brothers and Hans Christian Anderson. Hence, why I already had a Grimm's Fairy Tale book on my shelf to choose from.

My mama passed away right before I finally got to publish my first book, but I'm sure she is watching me.

As I usually do, I researched my project. Digging deep enough, I found a claimed base—where The Girl Without Hands originally came from—before the Grimm brothers made it their own. To honor the story, I kept some of the horrific tones and added my own spin. Hence, this serious warning.

A beautiful Alpha reader of mine told me that I may have to ask my readers to trust me on this one. That, early on, there was a point she wanted to stop reading, but took a leap of faith because she knows I always have a purpose.

I do.

And, if you keep reading, I promise there's a happy ending.

In this book, I push my characters to their limits. I pushed *my* limit. And, what has come of it—healing and beautiful deep breaths—and a sequel, The Man With A Treasure— I am grateful.

If you have serious triggers with rape or incest, *skip this story!*

If you wish to read on, remember… damaged souls are worth saving.

To those who can see no escape...

Hold on to the glimpses of light until you can find your way.

CHAPTER ONE

The Ruined One

Should a child cry out for her mother when the danger comes? Of course. But what if that mother is no more? What if she had been snuffed long ago and buried where the other bones lay? Her name was Isabella, and she was more beautiful than any of the queens in the fairytales she taught me how to read. Our days were long, sometimes ruthless, even if we only had each other.

For a beautiful while, she was able to hide from me our horrid truth - that we were captives of the cruelest of the cruel—darkest of the dark—with no chance of escape. Only death itself could set us free. When I was young enough to still be unaware of the true meaning of malice, I would swing on the swing set, in the wide sparse field behind the large home that I didn't yet view as the prison it was. No. Instead, I innocently stared at mountains off in the distance, unaffected by the madness taking place all around me. The tall brown and green grass was a buffer of sorts, sparing me from witnessing the gruesome acts my mother was being forced to endure.

The memories of the grunts and moans now haunt me for many reasons.

In the grass, hidden by nature, the pack of seven men would leave her behind so they could go and boast with each other about another 'wild fuck' with the daughter of a mafia king. None of their words struck my heart because, at the time, the syllables carried no meaning. My mother was still fighting hard to shield me—trying to find a way to save me—from a merciless future.

In fact, the men never appeared to me as humans. They felt like faceless moving shadows that stirred throughout the space around me. I knew they were older, but even at my young age, I was already blocking them out. Maybe, deep down, I sensed the danger that endlessly followed in their wake.

Once the pack of men went back inside, a worn woman with a brilliant soul would weakly drag herself from the tall grass, always thankful to see me waiting. At the time, I believed she was relieved because she adored me. I was clueless that she was thankful to still be the pack's main focus.

With her old summer dress torn and clutched in her trembling hands, Mother was covered with a white glue-like fluid still clinging to her skin, hair, reddened breasts, back, buttocks, thighs, and in between… "Scarlett," she would call out to me with a relieved kindness that should not belong to the scorned. "Would you please start the water?" English being her second language, she spoke with a foreign, regal tone that brought me comfort.

Having helped cleanse her many times before, I happily jumped from my swing to run to the outside spicket, more than willing to tend to the woman who loved me with her heart and soul. I cherished the moments the men weren't around. It meant I got my mother all to myself. When they were around, she usually stayed quiet and reserved. All I understood was that she wasn't telling me wonderful stories to pass the time.

With a full bucket of splashing water, I would return to the depleted woman who lay panting on her side. Gently and with great care, I would rinse her used body, unknowingly helping to bathe the shame away. Unaware of what I was touching, my soft little hands would scrub her clean. Then, once done, she would crawl to a dry spot on the ground and rest while I put away the bucket.

Upon returning, I would lie next to her, and we would stare at the sky. Snuggled to her side, I would ask, "What do you see in the clouds today, Mother?"

A breeze carrying mountain fresh air would blow through her drying black hair, that once shined like the horse on the cover of The Black Stallion book. "I see the angel of the night, waiting for the sun to fall, so he can come down to earth and find his Scarlett and take her away."

Her words held such feeling, but, unbeknownst to me, she was praying for the Angel of Death to come and collect her child. She'd rather me dead than to be in the pack's brutal grip.

My mother, Isabella Giordano, spoke with a thick accent of the Italian language I was forbidden to learn. Her 'roots' were not to be mine. The pack wanted no reminders that this daughter was tainted by the blood of an enemy. They didn't even like that my mother named me Scarlett; therefore, they would only refer to me as Scar or Little Shit. It didn't seem to matter that none of the men had any way of knowing who exactly my biological creator was, due to their constant rapes. Unified, they regarded me as *their* 'property,' and, no matter how many times my mother pleaded, they refused to 'sell' me.

Whenever I asked why she wanted me sold—an action I could not comprehend—my mother would whisper the only Italian she dared, "*Vita Mia*,"—My Life—"because, away from here, there is a chance for you to be *found*."

Found. One simple word with life-changing meaning.

Mother and I shared a small bed in a barren room. With bars on the one window we had, our view faced the mountains. Our door was always locked from the outside. I had a few crayons and coloring books, and every now and then, another fairytale book was thrown at us. I didn't know I was going without. I didn't know what the word abundance meant. I had never experienced a plethora of anything except my mother's love. My mother would hold me in her lap and read to me, pointing out the words to help me learn my letters.

Bath time was my favorite. In our adjoining bathroom, Mother would hold a plastic cup of water over my head and smile. "Okay, *Vita Mia*, close your eyes and pretend to be a *free* mermaid under a waterfall."

Giddy for the opportunity to use my imagination, I squealed and tilted my head back, eyes closed, ready to envision every page she had just read in one of my precious books. With my legs held together, I would wiggle them like a huge mermaid flipper, loving how my scales sparkled in the moonlight.

Since dinner wasn't usually brought to us, my mother would fill that same plastic bath cup and say, "Okay, *Vita Mia*, let's pretend you are drinking the most delicious soup, and it is filling your belly with a warmth that makes you sleepy and happy and ready to dream of the world waiting just for you."

Naïve, and luckily so, I would close my eyes and drink the warm water, imagining the full sensation in my belly. It would work. Happy and satisfied, I would yawn and crawl into bed without a complaint as rumbles of hunger echoed in our room. My mother would drink warm water, then join me, wrapping me tightly in her arms.

Sometimes, I was blessed and got to have her hold me all night long. Most of the time, late into the evening, she would be yanked from our bed and thrown to the floor, where my fathers would grope and undress her. Since it was common—all I had ever known— and my belly was full of warm water, I would sleep through much of it. As I got older—crossing from a toddler to a little girl, that became more challenging. I can't be sure of my age, because Mother lost track of the days and years that passed us by at its cruel pace, but I believe I was around the age of six when her struggles were no longer easy to overlook. Without my permission, my innocent ignorance began to slightly clear. Her cries became more noticeable. Her apparent suffering started tugging at my heart, even though I had never known my fathers to be kind. I never had an example of anything to compare their actions with.

The first night my fathers' routine attacks started truly scaring me, I cried out for her, not quite sure why my heart was racing.

During her horrid abuse on our bedroom floor, she endearingly told me, "*Vita*

Mia, go back to sleep."

I believed her false calm and closed my eyes, falling back asleep to the sound of her being struck by one of my fathers. *Whack!*

He warned, "Don't speak that Italian shit in this house."

Not being permitted to learn about my heritage was especially unkind, as the men who spawned me preferred that I not exist at all, but what they were doing to her was far worse.

When Mother spoke of her own father, tears would fall, and her ocean blue eyes would see beyond our prison walls. She would wish out loud, "Had only his hunger for more wealth not blinded him to the devil in disguise."

The devil had tricked my grandfather into believing he would bounty without a cost.

Now, as a woman with eyes wide open, *I* say, "To men who believe anything is free, may they lose their eyes and feet." That way they can continue to be blind, yet not have the ability to run from the price of their crimes. Just as my mother nor I could.

I believe I was almost seven years old when I awoke to mother sitting on top of my stomach one night, a knife in the air being held over my chest. Her eyes were squeezed shut, an agony-stricken face crying…

I whispered, "Mama?"

She gasped and snapped her eyes open. Then ultimate pity replaced her expression of dread. The knife slowly coming down to rest on the bed next to me, instead of in my chest, was her choice. I see that now. I understand her ultimate regret for not being stronger at the crucial moment, where my fate could have been altered for the better.

Her haunting whisper and cry are now embedded in my soul. "I am so sorry, *Vita Mia*. I have failed you. Your angel hasn't come, and I do not possess the will to bring you peace, even though I would happily be condemned to Hell for my sin. For you. For I love you, my daughter."

She knew. She knew of the appalling acts that were approaching, and tried to save me from becoming the next victim of the torture that had become her everyday life.

My mother tucked the knife under my pillow before lying next to me, pulling me close to her chest so we could fall asleep. "*Vita Mia*, if one of your fathers ever tries to lie here with you, you are to take this knife and sink it into his stomach."

I gasped. I had never raised a hand to a father, nor had I ever been physically close to one.

"I know," she patted my head, "but you need to promise me."

Scared and so confused, I vowed to use the blade.

I think she secretly hoped the disobedience would anger a father to the point he would kill me in rage. I think she hoped they would snuff out my life, where she couldn't.

When I was much older, there would be many a time I would be angry at her moment of weakness, wishing that blade would have taken me from this earth…

Soon after that, my fathers took Isabella Giordano from our room and never brought her back to me. I cried for her. I cried so long, I believe it's all I did for days and days…

I was surprised by the smell of a father as he crawled into bed with me, waking me from slumber. His breath was sharp to my delicate nose. His weight was so much more than my mother's. His touch lacked her gentleness.

Never having hurt anyone before, or even seen a movie to know how hard to stab with a knife, I barely punctured his skin. I was so young, and so inexperienced. How was I supposed to know how to be violent?

After that, everything as I knew it tumbled away. Just like my innocence as it was stolen by the very same father. Two of us bled on that bed that night.

How do grown men find gratification in sexual encounters with little girls? I don't think I will ever have that answer. Fortunately, not all of the fathers were interested in me at such a young age. With the couple that were, I quickly surrendered to them because the pain was much less when I didn't resist.

After being physically hurt, my childhood swing set felt different the next time I was allowed to be outside. I was too inexperienced to understand what was happening, but everything around me felt altered. It was almost as if, even though sexual abuse was common practice, due to what I had witnessed my mother endure all my life, deep down, my heart still knew something was wrong. Idaho's mountains seemed farther away, as if the rest of the world I had heard about was fading from my memory. The tall grass around me no longer looked like a shield, but a promise of a grim future to come. An alternate future was inconceivable since I knew nothing else.

More children and women appeared in the house from time to time. I could hear cries and sometimes screams while I huddled in my bed. I even shared my mattress when some kids were tossed into my room, until they, too, were taken away and never returned. Just like my mother.

I don't know what changed, or why I was soon no longer being taken out of my room, but I never saw my swing set again. Nor was I ever able to be outside of the dilapidated home. In fact, there would only be a number of times that I would see beyond my bedroom. Then my end would come, once and for all.

Eventually, I lost more things I would sorely miss. As my body grew and could no longer fit into my little girl clothing, I was offered no new clothes. Soon in a constant state of nakedness, and no longer with children in my room, my only visitors were more fathers.

As I developed, so did their hunger.

It's sad, but I was so lonely, I wished they would talk to me as they used my body. They didn't. At least nothing as wonderful as my mother's stories, that is. Here and there, I would get foul words shared, such as, "Ah shit, that feels so fucking good," or, "Oh yeah, this tight little hole is just what I needed after my fucked-up day".

When my menstrual cycle began and I was scared of the unusual blood, I didn't get an explanation about my body transforming into a woman. I simply was told, "Stick these in your cunt so you stop bleeding everywhere."

"I'm not sick?" I asked, confused by the changes my body was experiencing.

Washcloths were tossed at me. "No, you dumb shit."

That's why, when my belly began to grow beyond my bare ribs, I again thought I was sick, but all I got was, "Jesus." And, "We knocked her up!" And, "Fuck."

Delivering my child was a ghastly experience. It was pain like never before, and that was a vile statement considering what I had endured up to this point in my life. Even though I was unaware what the fathers were doing to me was 'bad,' per se, it still hurt. I quickly learned my pain was not important, only their pleasure.

At the young age of twelve, I was left all alone in the bathroom. I was not permitted to get out of the old pink tub. They hadn't appreciated the 'mess' I was leaving on the bathroom floor as my body prepared for the birth.

"Help me," I cried to deaf ears.

The fathers couldn't have cared less about my horrendous labor—a young body trying to deliver another human while so malnourished it was a sin.

In all my life, I had never watched TV or read an adult book of any kind. Therefore, I had no knowledge of childbirth. That's why, my stomach twisting as if the infant trying to be born was wielding many blades, I was filled with terror. "Help me," I cried out again, my voice echoing against solitary walls.

Watching blood seeping toward the drain, I was sure I wouldn't survive. My body forced me to bare down, and I believed my end had come, like a character from a book Mother once read to me.

When an infant finally broke free from between my thighs, my body found instant relief. He slipped toward the drain as I sunk back against the cold tub, trying to regain awareness. My mind spun as my body attempted to adjust to no longer housing another human, although I didn't understand that at the time. The lightheaded sensation was only cleared by a cry I had never heard before.

I knew little of mothering, except for the care my own mother gave me. How was I supposed to know how to treat an infant when never having seen one before? Even though my education was grossly limited, and I was clueless about how babies were born, common sense had me quickly realizing I was staring at a baby.

My mother had spoken of instincts and how important it was that I followed them.

So, that's what I did.

My heart, my gut, and my aching arms insisted I pick up the newborn and offer it warmth, in an embrace only a mother could offer.

"Scarlett," my mother's voice echoed in my mind. *"Would you please start the water?"*

Holding my baby close, I leaned forward and ran the water until it was warm, then cupped the cleansing fluid in my palm. My plastic cup had broken long ago. I missed it dearly. Gently, I dripped the water over my son, who would come to be named... *Seth.*

CHAPTER TWO

After the birth, and because I had gone so quiet, a father checked on us. He peeked in the tub. "A boy? Huh. That's better than what your mother gave us."

Wet, cold, bleeding, and exhausted, I peered up at the man who found what 'my mother gave him' to be a special treat for his body to enjoy as he pleased. I think it was the first time I felt anger toward a father.

He lifted a brow in warning. "Scar, you want me to stick that bastard in the toilet and flush?"

Seth was so tiny, I assumed it was possible. My arms tightened around the infant as I quickly began to understand my mother's actions. She hadn't been weak not fighting my fathers. She had been *strong* by trying to protect me.

He sneered, "Exactly," then started walking away.

"Wait," I dared to call out because I was already caring and fearful for my son's well-being. "What do I feed him?"

"That shit leaking out of your tits."

Seth—my premature baby—and I had beautifully tender moments between a son and mother. In between those moments were trials and errors, but he made them all worthwhile. I endlessly gave and gave to him all I could. Kisses and hugs…

I drank plenty of water from the faucet so I could keep producing milk. It had barely been enough for me to survive. Now, only receiving food once a day was even worse. I rapidly lost weight from nursing him, but kept giving because he made my heart so full.

I was no longer alone.

Not familiar with diapers, I didn't think to ask for any. Not that the fathers would have obliged. With my clean menstrual washcloths, I did my best to create a place for Seth to soil.

Instead of appreciating their son, or treasuring him as I did, the fathers prevented more children. I was put on birth control as soon as I was finished bleeding from giving birth. I also received a couple of baby garments that took a long time for Seth to grow into, due to his concerning size. Razors were provided to me to 'clean up' the hole that I 'ruined' with my son.

As my fathers had done to my mother, they used Seth against me. Not that I ever fought them, but they could get me to do anything they wanted if I could keep my child. They seemed to feed off my desperation to not lose the only being I had in my world.

By the age of approximately thirteen—my body was fully developing—and no fathers held back on their sexual needs. At that time, I was only spared dealing with them all at once. Having them all at once would not have been viewed, by me, as a horrendous circumstance. Again, it was all I knew—what I had witnessed my mother undergo.

Because she somehow successively kept me from becoming damaged with all I had seen and had me believe there was no foul play, I believed Seth would grow up to be just like me. Unmarked. After all, he was only being exposed to what I had seen for years—horrors I didn't recognize as horrors.

What I had no way of comprehending, being raised in such an environment, was all my mother's prior experiences before she had been abducted. How her knowledge influenced her actions and made her capable of controlling my perception of the rapes taking place in plain sight. She had once been a woman living in a world I had never known; therefore, she had tools I had yet to possess or know.

Besides what brought my body physical pain, I wasn't aware of the effects of seeing a significant amount of abuse or how it could be detrimental to one's mental well-being. I was blind to how *I* had already been affected, thinking this way was a clear sign of my damaged perception.

Having no knowledge of how my son would be affected if the man who biologically fathered me, also biologically spawned him, was also a hindrance. Or how much damage was caused to Seth by me being so malnourished during my whole pregnancy. Not to mention the premature birth with no medical assistance.

After one of my fathers was done having sex with me, he noticed Seth sitting on the dirty carpet. Getting dressed, he lifted his chin. "Why does he do that?"

Seth, now a year old, often sat on the floor with the tip of his finger drawing a continuous circle around himself. The process would entertain him for hours on end.

Concerned by the question, I sat up on the bed. "Do all kids not do this?"

His upper lip snarled. "It sure don't look right." He eyed me. "Did you do something to him?"

Appalled, I gasped, clueless to any harm I may have caused. "I don't know. Did I?"

"Damn, you're dumb as hell." Blowing off any concern he should've had, he shrugged. "Maybe he wants a train set or something."

Now, my eyes widened for a different reason. I had never seen a train set in real life.

That father had been correct about our son. Seth was different from average children. He was walking by seven months and potty trained by eleven. He didn't talk. He didn't call me Mama like the children in books my mother had read to me.

Without the true experience of being a mother or witnessing more mothers in action, it was too late by the time I realized something was wrong with my child, although there was nothing I could've done to change the outcome.

It was the way Seth would sit so still, watching, staring, as if studying everything going on around him. I would try to hold the toddler in my lap and read to him, like my mother so affectionately did to me, but he would crawl out of my lap to sit on the floor and go back to drawing circles around where he sat with his finger.

How the fathers had not lost interest in my body was bewildering to me, but the older I got, the more their interest grew. They didn't seem to 'like' me much but didn't carry the same hatred they carried for my mother. They even made comments on my beauty and body, how my hair was black as night, my skin as light as snow, and my flared lips red like a ruby.

Internally, I smiled, proud to look like my mother.

In my bedroom, I would tell my little boy to go play with his train set as I was surrounded by all my fathers. I believed I was now seventeen and learning a little of what my mother had tolerated. Several of my fathers' organs would penetrate me at once. My mouth. My vagina. My anus. The rest would fondle me or themselves.

Sadly, and somewhat pathetically, I was thankful to not be in need of muffling cries as my mother did. When they ganged up on me like they used to her, it wasn't quite as brutal, hostile. Or maybe, because I knew no better and had been undergoing rapes for over a decade, years longer than what she had suffered, I didn't see the destruction being done to my body or spirit.

I guess the 'damaged' find encouraging thoughts wherever they can.

Tears would eventually be mine, though, in a very unexpected form.

Asleep in bed one night about a year later, I woke to a very unfamiliar touch. To this day, I still can't shake what I saw. Seth was sitting between my legs, touching my vagina with his toy train.

I may have not known much due to the way I was raised. I may have become accustomed to the atrocity of being forced to have sex with my fathers, but my son touching me in that manner rocked me to my core. The revulsion in my heart and soul was as powerful as an erupting volcano, icing over in only one second.

I can't recall racing from the bed. I can't recall how I ended up sitting in a corner on the floor, staring at the little boy who still sat on the bed, watching me. His expression was… void.

If my mother wanted me to protect myself against the fathers touching me like that, what would she have thought of my son? Would she want him to be stabbed, too?

I hadn't even realized I had wailed out in horror until the bedroom door opened and a father demanded, "What the fuck is wrong with you?"

"I…" I pointed to my son, who now felt like an unknown danger. "He…"

"Speak!"

"He touched me!"

"So?"

I pointed to between my thighs.

"No shit?" My father actually smiled, gazing back at the child as if the boy was finally becoming something he could be proud of.

To my dismay, he left, only to return with the rest of my fathers. They all circled, curious as to what was happening.

The father that discovered me earlier in the corner, where I was still, now stood pointing. "Our Seth here felt up his mom."

Sensing impending danger, I pulled my legs close to my chest.

"*What?*" squawked a father. "He's like, what, five?"

"Hey! Maybe he's *my* kid, after all!"

"I've been fucking her for *years* longer than you. He's totally my kid."

How this was something to be celebrated is another facet I may never understand, but celebrate they did.

After they had proof.

Besides when I had been seven, I had never felt so violated as I did while being held down by them all. I roared, spit like an animal, and fought to be set free, but my weak and malnourished body was no challenge for seven men.

Cemented to the ground by fourteen brutal hands, my legs were held apart.

A father called out, "Hey, Seth, come show us what you like to do with your train."

Tears rushed from my eyes, and I was filled with terror as my son climbed down from the bed, train clutched in his little hand. "No, Seth!" I screamed, "No! Go back to bed."

The child was focused, and it was wasn't on my words.

Staring at the moldy ceiling, not daring to watch the unthinkable happen, I screamed, wanting to be heard so terribly it felt like my heart was being held so it could not beat. Maybe I was begging it to stop pumping blood, so I could die before my son touched me—before I would be altered, becoming a woman that would be riddled with such anguish she would never completely recover.

As it had happened my whole life, once my mother was gone, no one came to help me or listened to what I had to say. The tip of the train banged against my core and heart, simultaneously. Madly, I kept screaming, so loud I could barely hear them all laughing and encouraging my son to touch his mother. I screamed… as little fingers did.

CHAPTER THREE

The Mad One

Some actions by others can be too much from which to recover…

When Seth touched me that night, I learned what caused true nightmares. I kept screaming, no matter what was said or done by any father of mine. Even when the train was removed from between my thighs, it was too late. All the years of mistreatment had violently risen from my heart and damaged spirit. There'd been no story my mother read or told me where a child should view his mother in such a manner. The fundamental part of my being recognized this tainted violation, therefore having me doubt all I had believed to be true.

As my belief system discovered cracks in its foundation—that all of what my fathers had been doing to me might be wrong—the obedient part of me they had created started to crumble.

Mentally. Physically. Emotionally.

And replacing what had once been, was… rage.

This caged animal went rabid. I hit. I swung at any father within my reach. Seth didn't cry as his mother lost all sense of her human traits. He just stayed behind a father who was trying to shield him from my madness, as they all fled my bedroom.

Alone, my fury did not simmer. It strengthened.

What few items I had were shredded. My mattress—the ultimate symbol of my being raped, not a place to sleep—was tossed on its side in a different corner. My one window shattered against my wrath. That's when the fathers rushed back in, my son no longer with them, and tied me up.

Sure to stay far from my mouth, which was trying to bite anyone close to me, they rolled me to my side and picked me up like a log.

Stranger's eyes—children and women—watched as the fathers carried me through the house I hadn't seen in years and dragged me down wooden steps into a cold basement. I didn't care. I kept roaring, unable to communicate the injustice my life had been since I was born because no one taught me how.

Even with what my son had done, I knew he was innocent. I desperately wanted to hold him and forgive him. I wanted to see the little boy in him, not the monster his fathers were making him. Once thrown in the empty room, the door slammed shut and locked, I banged on it, fiercely wanting them to return my child to me.

I was refused, and the fathers only visited when they were up for a challenge.

Months later…

A snarl burned in my throat as I heard their heavy steps. The aged wooden stairs had become my alarm to danger. As the door swung open, with the rusty hinges announcing the unwanted arrival, I faced the pack of seven and smiled with a vengeance. I knew it may not be mine that day, nor the next, but as I glared at the men ready to take me, I knew someday, somehow, their deaths would be mine.

One of my possible fathers cooed with pleasure, "Oh, Scar is ready to *play,* boys."

My toes gripped the cold floor, my knees bent. My hands widened, ready to scratch and claw all the skin I could find until they bound me. "Let me see my *child*."

Yes, if the fathers wished to fuck, it was a fight like they had never seen in me. I didn't even know that courage existed, but there it was. A lioness in the girl who looked like Snow White. I battled them with all my might, even if only weaponed with my hands.

Unfortunately, even those would be taken away. They would cheer and mock my pain, tying my wrists together, then string me up from the ceiling. The rope strangling my wrists was looped through rings attached to the ceiling. The end of the rope tied to a hook by the basement door so that they could release me from afar.

With my feet tied apart, I would stare up at my bound hands that felt as if I had none due to the lack of circulation. Below, my body was savaged at their will.

It may be believed that tears are only made of water… but I can assure you, they are made of so much more. Grief, loss, heartache, and pain is what the magic fluid is made of. And that agony dripped from my face and my spirit that somehow still fought to live.

At the entrance to the basement, the last father to leave me stood there, untying the end of the rope. "Got any fight left in you, Scar?"

Hanging from the ceiling, my legs now untied but barely functional, I refused to dignify him with an answer. I only let out a growl to remind him of the beast they had awakened in me, even though I was physically drained from the gang rape.

He sighed. "I do miss that mouth on my dick."

Once I had become an uncontrollable animal, none of the fathers dared to stick anything of value into my mouth.

Wise choice.

There was no reservation left in me. My teeth would have happily severed anything, bloody or not.

When the rope loosened, I fell to the ground.

The overhead lights were turned off and the door closed. Only the light from the bathroom shined on me.

With hands still bound, I was relieved to no longer be hanging from the ceiling. More tears dripped to the cold floor as I stared at my bleeding wrists, the present rope giving no reprieve to the stinging injuries. The rest of my skin was drenched with semen, making the cold cement floor even more unbearable. Loneliness seeped deep into my heart, one that was begging for an ounce of kindness.

And… I missed my son. I missed holding him. I missed giving his cheek kisses. I missed feeling his warmth, even as he would eventually pull from all my embraces.

With my hands tied, I pushed to my weak legs, stumbling into the bathroom, the long rope dragging behind me.

"Scarlett?" my mother's past voice haunted me. *"Would you please start the water?"*

"Yes, Mother."

Once the water in the shower ran wonderfully warm, I stepped under the stream and tilted my head back, letting it cleanse me like I used to cleanse my mother. More tears fell as I imagined myself being that beautiful mermaid, basking in the moonlight, my mother's hands gently pouring warm water from my cup over my head.

Slowly, I turned to the water and opened my mouth, drinking until the warm soup filled my empty and depleted belly.

After the shower, I did my best to dry the ropes around my wrists. The pain would always slip away faster if I could keep the injuries dry. I made my way back into the basement and laid on the cold floor. I stared at the door, hoping to see my son being returned to me, but that wouldn't happen.

He was theirs now.

The visits became fewer, the rapes farther apart.

The mad struggle that I refused to end when they were near me ultimately became my own hero. I guess they didn't possess the dedication I did. They only wanted a hole to degrade and belittle.

With my hands always tied to a rope, I stayed locked away in that basement for so long I witnessed myself age...

The basement is where I was to stay until my death angel came for me.

Years later...

The basement door creaked open, and a package was thrown in. "Shave and clean yourself up. We're finally selling your stupid ass."

Sold...

My heart lit up. This is what my mother had always hoped for. Feeling my first glimpse of hope, ever, I took the items and rushed into the bathroom. I was so desperate to be free of the basement, I was willing to clean or shave any part of myself for the chance to leave.

Seth.

As I shampooed my hair, I wondered what he looked like now. I wondered if I could convince the one who was to buy me, to buy him, too. My eyes filled with happy tears as I pictured Seth and I out in the field by the swing set. I couldn't imagine beyond that because I had never been anywhere.

As I brushed my teeth, with toothpaste this time since it was finally offered, I wondered if Seth had a beautiful smile.

Dry and naked, I stood in the basement, waiting. I looked around, wondering if this would be my last day in the lonely and wretched room. Then I quickly rushed forward and put the end of my rope in the hook by the door so my fathers would know I wouldn't fight this sale. That I would behave.

I had even turned on the light so they could see I was clean and presentable.

Then I waited… for what seemed like days…

Laughter echoed down the stairs before I heard footfalls on the steps. A father was telling someone, "She is a little bit on the wild side, but definitely unworldly like you're looking for. I hear you have been searching for some time?"

My Angel of Death's voice was mature, steady, and with a faint hint of an accent that I somehow recognized. "So far, there has not been what I… *need.*" The determination he voiced in one word made me pray he would be the answer my mother had hoped for.

"For the price you're willing to spend, I sure hope Scar is the one for you."

The stranger sounded frustrated. "I am hungry to return home with the prize that has been most elusive so far."

Not knowing what elusive meant, my head fell forward. I was sure I wasn't that. I believed I was nothing of value. *My only chance may come and go… without me.*

When the door finally opened, I sucked air and unmanageable hope into my lungs. With my head still hanging forward, my long hair drifted in front of me, dancing in my heavy breaths of nerves.

Without looking up, I listened as my father noticed my rope, waiting as eagerly as me. "Hmm. How about that. It seems someone's ready to behave today."

Staring at the cold floor beneath me, hoping to know warmth once again, I let my tied wrists be lifted above me.

"You have to keep her restrained like this?" asked the Mature One.

"Eh, only if you like to keep your dick attached."

"I will approach her alone. Thank you." The Mature One spoke with a discipline I had never known. He was refined and in charge without demanding a damn thing. His voice carried a warning that I was too naïve to recognize. The newfound animal in me decided her best line of defense was to do as he wished.

So, I did.

As his dress shoes clicked on the floor, he asked, "Your name," without making the words sound like a question. Only another demand.

Yet to have the strength to lift my head, due to being afraid I would waste away in the basement, I spoke through my curtain of black hair. "Scarlett." I studied the dark dress slacks that appeared in my line of sight.

Even though the Mature One had been warned about my previous actions, the bold man confidently reached out and touched the tips of my very long hair. He had a gold ring on his right hand that shined in the light as the tips of his fingers caressed my hair as if inspecting. "Do you like the name Scar?"

"My mother did not call me that name."

His ringed hand released my hair then reached up under it, slowly coming toward my hidden face. It was as if he knew not to spook the animal on display. When the backside of his hand finally touched my chin, his thumb came to my mouth. Testing me, it gently rubbed over my open lips, my nervous breath caressing his skin.

He smelled of soap and the cleanest water. It made me think of the waterfall I imagined when I needed to escape. He also had another scent I couldn't place, but instantly appreciated. I hoped it was the scent of the magical moon I was sure was somewhere close, shining down on me.

When I didn't nip as he was told I would, his hand found the side of my face and held me. I had not been touched like this since my mother. Maybe that is why his gentle touch had me obeying and leaning into his palm. Maybe that is why the same thumb that had just stroked my lips now caught the one tear that dripped from me…
Please take us with you.

The Mature One spoke to someone else who I wasn't even aware was in the room. "Sal, move five thousand dollars into his account as good-faith and for him to leave this room."

A velvety deep voice echoed, "Yes, sir."

After a pause, a father laughed in astonishment. "You could've had a go at her for free, but thanks. It's already in the account. Hopefully, there will be a million more soon." The door shut, and then I heard heavy steps moving up the wooden stairs.

None of the talk about 'accounts' and 'million' made sense to me, so I was afraid these were all bad signs. I wondered if the Mature One could hear the thundering in my chest. I was in such despair, knowing I could take no more of my captivity. Even if I was only trading one for another, at least there was a hope to feel the sun on my skin once more.

The Mature One didn't move. He only held my cheek. "Scarlett, my next question is a very important one."

A sob broke from my aching soul as I nodded.

"What was your mother's name?"

Just thinking about her, my eyes closed and my lungs expanded, almost as if her ghost was with me in spirit. "It was *Isabella*."

The other man—Sal's—dress shoes began to pace at my answer,

The Mature One slowly lifted my chin, having my hair fall from my face. With my head now tilted back, almost between my restrained arms, my face resting in his hands, he spoke, "Scarlett, may I see your eyes for confirmation?"

I didn't know the meaning of that word either, but so far, he had shown me nothing but kindness. So, I let my last bit of hope carry me through, and I opened my eyes.

As I said before, I can't recall the details of my fathers' faces. They were simply… men. The only ones I'd ever known. I didn't study them. I only survived them. But, when a new face appeared, I soaked in every one of his details and saw he was everything they weren't. His face was bold. Powerful. Thick cheekbones and a determined chin couldn't be covered by his short-trimmed beard. His deep, dark eyes full of mystery and retribution widened as they stared down at me. Tightly cut hair as black as mine had me wanting to reach out and touch it.

The Mature One was younger than my fathers, but so much cleaner. His breath wasn't sharp. His touch wasn't angry. His trembling smile wasn't promising punishment. His words weren't full of cruelty…

"*Vita Mia*."

The ringing in my ears was so simultaneous, I was sure someone had hit me across the face, just as my fathers had. I stuttered, "W-What did you say?"

In Italian, he whispered something so beautiful it sounded like a prayer.

I was sad to miss the translation. "I-I don't understand what you are saying."

The Mature One said no more. He only stared at me as if I were a ghost, like my mother.

So, loudly, I begged, "Please, tell me—"

"Shh!" The taller man with lighter hair, Sal, reached over my head with a pocketknife and sawed at the rope, whispering, "He said, 'I thought this day would never come'."

CHAPTER FOUR

The Mature One

Scarlett stole my breath when her blue eyes opened. They were layered with a tragic past, an undetermined present, a waning future. Her soul instantly spoke to mine through the tear still on my thumb, telling me we had found her just in time. This gruesomely tortured being was giving up. She was epically at the end of two ropes. One that had her bound to a life I would no longer let her live, and one that was barely convincing her to hold on mentally.

So many years had passed during the search for our Giordano princess that I could barely comprehend she was finally standing in front of me. Having no pictures or proof she even existed anymore, I had studied her mother's portrait to the point that I had become infatuated with a girl I had yet to meet. I knew, beyond a shadow of a doubt, if Scarlett looked even slightly like her mother did by a certain age, I would recognize her by touch alone. From under her magnificent black hair, as soon as I touched her full lips that flared, I knew I had found her.

While that pathetic man was still in the basement, it took much restraint to hide my inner response—my elation that I would soon rescue this Italian treasure from the despicable captivity that was slowly killing her grandfather by way of grief.

Once Sal's knife cut through the rope attached to the ceiling, Scarlett's arms fell forward and around my neck. Studying me, she asked, "W-Who are you?"

I am the one who will never fail you. "I am *Angelo*; Angel."

Her perfect mouth fell open, then those rosy lips began to tremble. "She said… the angel of the night would come."

My *il Compagno*—buddy, Sal Rossi, stopped his nervous examination of Scarlett's dreary living quarters to study my black suit then quietly spoke in Italian, "*I see no cameras, but let us make this quick, no?*"

His alarm told me he was well aware of who I had in my hands and that time was of the essence. "Yes," I kept staring into the eyes of a true angel, so unlike my criminal self, "let us leave with Isabella *Giordano's* daughter."

Scarlett had not told me her mother's last name, so I let my Italian accent temporarily appear, then waited for her certainty to register.

Water collected and danced in the blues I would never forget, even after death. They were like staring into the galaxy of planets and stars.

"M-My… mother?"

"Yes." It took me a second or two to respond because I felt as though I was under a spell, losing track of time altogether. "She is alive."

After years in captivity by her new owners, Isabella was finally rescued. It was my father, head of Mr. Giordano's security, that was the one who found her in Australia. She was beyond damaged. Between the abuse and drugs she had become addicted to, it took a long time for her mind to properly operate.

The Giordano family was horrified once they learned Isabella had birthed a child while in captivity…

With the news of her mother still being alive, I knew Scarlett was going to faint before she did. Since she was significantly underweight, I easily caught her limp body, then held her in a cradle of affection and respect, no matter her present condition. "Sal, your jacket." I wanted her naked body covered.

"*Angelo*," warned my comrade in Italian. "*Do not fuck this up by showing anything other than the disregard any man buying a damaged woman would have.*" He pointed to her wrist. "*I must leave her tied to show lack of respect.*"

My nostrils flared as my eyes slid shut in frustration. Italian women in my life were held so high. Now, I had to treat one as if she were simply a piece of meat from the local butchers.

Fighting my disgust, I gave a quick nod.

Sal quietly added, "*Removing her while unconscious may be kind. Who knows if she is friends with any of those pour souls up there?*"

No matter how many trafficking establishments we had visited over the years, secretly looking for Scarlett while under the ruse I was searching for a woman who was of a certain nature, we saw the condition sex slaves had been living in ran from foul to ghastly. Some places 'turn and burn' their product. Others use and torture because it's not only about money for them. They seem to truly find pleasure in the torment and process of breaking down the human spirit.

Sal and I had to leave some of the victims to suffer and be sold. If we had revealed their whereabouts to authorities, it wouldn't have been long before Sal and I would no longer be invited to future establishments out of suspicion alone. We couldn't afford any circumstances that could be associated with us. So, we left behind a false trail as the only clue about when another mission was unsuccessful. We also continued to spread the word of what we were looking for—a woman who had been raised in captivity and was not worldly.

Once to the States, we caught word of a certain group of men having an 'animal' tied up in the basement. With enough money offered, we were able to make contact.

In the basement, I shivered, thinking about what we saw when arriving. I growled, "*What that boy was doing to that young woman—*"

Sal held up a hand, begging me to stop. "*With a toy train? I will never be the same.*"

The boy had been evil reincarnated. Never had I seen such cruelty in such a young person. The young woman being tortured was forcibly being held down by men that were weak-minded and controlled by drugs, egos, and unhealthy desires. The seven men in charge were undisciplined animals with no trainer. Weapons and cocaine had been lying about on tables and counters as proof.

Apparently, the young woman being molested had a friend. The friend was an older boy, barely older than the abuser, and was screaming for everyone to leave her alone. The pain on his face as he fought his chain, trying to reach her, was beyond horrific.

Positive Scarlett had experienced such terror while in the hands of the despicable, I gave one quick, adoring glance to her before becoming the man that must appear as one with the low morals as to purchase a woman. I knew it wouldn't be easy. Now holding her, my obsession multiplied. *"Sal, lift her arms, please."*

Sal whispered to our unconscious princess, *"Perdonami,"*—forgive me—then lifted her arms as I moved her body to crudely hang over my shoulder. When her bare ass laid exposed at my chest, Sal quickly diverted his eyes away.

Grateful for his discretion and his sound advice to protect Scarlett, I faced the door. "Transfer the money." I had only been in the basement with dim lighting for mere moments and already desired the sun. How pale Scarlett was, I was certain she hadn't experienced the sun in years.

Sal raced his fingers over his satellite phone, then said, "Done."

We waited for the transaction to hit our enemies' account. Could we have flown in support from Italy to kill all involved? Yes, but that was never the plan. Retribution would take place *after* our *Giordano* treasure was safe. Handing over a million dollars for her recovery was never an amount to dispute. We were given limitless reserves.

In the basement, one by one, Sal pulled each of his guns from under his suit jacket and double-checked them in case our arrangement was not to be honored. Balancing Scarlett on my right shoulder, I did the same to my own guns. We were both prepared to die to rescue the woman in our care. We were, and had been, that committed. It was imperative we succeed. I had a desperate mother waiting to hold the girl she hadn't seen for almost two decades.

Once an ample amount of time passed, I head-gestured for Sal to open the door and lead the way. As soon as the old wooden door was opened, we could hear cheering from upstairs. I assumed they had already been alerted to the purchase price now in the appointed bank account. But I was wrong.

Young bodies were huddled in dark corners of the small living room, all tied to furniture or hooks bolted to the walls. The curtains were drawn, and the odor was offensive. Buckets with feces were an indication the sex slaves were not taken to the bathroom often.

The seven crude men were now all on their feet, huddled, pointing, and laughing in the dirty kitchen. I didn't want to trail past them with Scarlett so exposed, nor through the kitchen because that is where the teenage girl had been chained to a stove, but I had to in order to reach the front door. The young woman was now sitting against the wall, her young friend sitting between her naked legs while facing the men. He had ripped his confinement from the wall and ran to the girl, his blue eyes spilling hatred. By his bleeding mouth and face, I knew he had just received quite a beating for his misbehavior, but he was still determined to protect his female friend.

She was crying, holding him back, telling the men, "He'll stop! Please! No more! I will make him stop!" The young man only had on jeans and had cigarette burns, old and new, on his chest.

Sitting next to the both of them, totally unfocused on anyone or anything but his train, was the boy. He had a bloody lip himself but still seemed unfazed. He just kept licking the toy as if it were merely an ice-cream cone.

My stomach turned as I fought a cringe at the sight, and said, "Men, the money has been transferred."

They turned to face me, all smiles and talking at the same time.

"Oh, you liked you some Scar, eh?"

"That pussy used to be so tight."

"Her ass still is!"

"And that tongue, I sure will miss that mouth."

As I took a step forward while reaching for my gun, Sal stepped in front of me again. "My boss has a plane to catch. Could you please confirm you have received payment so we may be on our way?"

One of the older crude men grumbled, "Rich people talk funny."

Another man boasted at his satellite phone, "Damn that bank account is fat!"

Sal gestured for me to start walking toward the door while thanking the men. "My boss will be sure to highly recommend you to certain acquaintances."

Walking past them, Sal following, I thought we had succeeded, but Scarlett woke up. Groggily, her head lifted from my back. "Seth?" Then her body jolted, her hands pushing against my back to see. "Seth! No! Drop the train!" She spoke to the young demented boy as if she knew him well. I was quite confused. That is why I didn't have good enough sense to stop Scarlett when she dropped from my shoulder.

Sal was as baffled as I. We simply couldn't comprehend the worry in Scarlett's voice when it came to the most horrid child we had ever encountered. He literally made us shake, positive he was the spawn of the devil.

That's how she easily got past us both to run back toward the boy she kept calling Seth. The menacing child didn't react to her, just kept licking his toy.

The men all started laughing. One even said, "He's staying with us, Scar."

Slightly recovering, I rushed toward her. She was already kneeling on the ground in front of the boy, trying to take the toy from him as if it were deadly, but her tied hands made it difficult. As soon as she saw me coming, she pleaded, "He must come with us—"

The way she was talking to me was far too revealing of who I truly was, so I did all I could to not to risk this rescue. I smacked her across the face so hard she flew into the two huddled teenagers. Her tied hands made it impossible to catch herself.

More laughter roared from the men behind me. Taking advantage of the distraction, I bent over to collect a dazed and confused Scarlett, hoping she would someday forgive me.

The teenage girl with haunting grey eyes somehow recognized my remorse. It was as if she could read my mind. When I scooped up Scarlett, the grey-eyed girl whispered, "Steel Stallions."

I had no idea what that meant, nor did I dare ask. The Giordano in my arms was my priority.

It's possible that my infatuation with Scarlett started turning into a love of sorts at that very moment because, as I lifted her from the ground, her hand caressed the young woman, and she whispered, "Found. You will be found." Her sincerity, like her eyes, spoke to my soul.

As the men's laughter finally settled, I thanked them for their fine 'slave' and walked out of the dirtiest and most heartbreaking of all the places I was forced to visit.

In my arms, with her hands still tied, Scarlett shielded her eyes from the sunlight. Sal and I squinted, but refused to slow our brisk walk toward the blue Mercedes. Sal opened the back door and quickly shut it as soon as I sat with Scarlett, firm in my embrace. I didn't seem to possess the will to release her. As Sal rushed around the back of the car, I whispered, "I am so sorry to have struck you."

Reacting as if being hit was something she was completely accustomed to, she explained, "Punishments come when I misbehave."

Sal had no sooner opened the driver's door before he was in and starting the engine.

Eyes still covered due to discomfort, Scarlett jumped. "W-What is that?"

Confused, I blinked. "Just the engine."

"What is a 'engine'?"

Scarlett not knowing the correct way to say '*an* engine' was a telling sign of her lack of education. Her not even knowing what one was, was a cold reminder of where we just stole her from.

Sal had tires spinning and us racing down the long dirt driveway. Scarlett, blinded by the light, had arms flailing at the movement. "What is happening?" Her eyes watered as she tried to force them open.

Driving at a high speed, Sal told me, *"Angelo, I do not think she has ever been in a car."*

With considerable strength, I pulled Scarlett close to my chest, shielding her face in the crook of my neck. "Shh. Rest your eyes."

Her alarmed breathing hit my skin, but Scarlett did lean into me, accepting the shelter for her sensitive eyes. "They burn."

I leaned my head to hers to offer more shelter and comfort. "They will adjust."

"Adjust?"

Sadness pelted my heart. English was my second language, yet I knew more than this poor soul who was, technically, American. "With patience, your eyes will get used to the beautiful sun."

"When I was a child, I loved the sun. It didn't hurt me then."

"It will stop hurting you again. I promise."

She sighed, her weight melting into me even more until Sal took a sharp turn out of the driveway. Scarlett's tied hands flew out as if to catch herself. There was no denying how she moved them in unison, which told me they had been bound together for a very long time.

Pulling her scarred hands to my chest, I promised, "I won't let you fall. You are safe." Then I growled to Sal, *"I want the ropes off her."*

"I want us far from the hell hole."

After she settled some, and there was a moment of silence except for the roaring engine, Scarlett said, "Seth is my son."

Sal's eyes raced to mine in the rearview mirror. Then he grumbled, *"There is no soul in her son."*

With regret, because Sal was speaking the truth, I nodded but got distracted when noticing Scarlett grabbing her stomach. I tried to divert her attention. "Have you ever seen the mountains you have lived in?" Hidden in my neck still, she nodded. "Someday you will get the chance to see them like a bird can."

She gasped with an innocence that was heartbreaking coming from a woman in her twenties. "In the air?"

"Yes. We can fly. Almost like them."

"I'm scared. I don't know how to fly."

Finally off the human trafficker's property, Sal raced down another dirt road. The only home Scarlett had ever known was buried deep in the Idaho mountains, hours from civilization. I craved concrete—any sign that we were getting her farther away from a place that was tragic and brutal.

I had been hired due to the hunting skills my father taught me and a promise I made long ago. I was hired because I am ruthless and very willing to kill, not because I possess much humanity anymore. Men I had murdered in the past had deserved the ill treatment I brought them. Young children and women in captivity? Only their ignorance and innocence were their enemy. Not me. So, I did my best to stay patient for Scarlett. "Just as Sal is driving this car, another man will fly our plane."

"Angel—"

The roads became winding, quickly proving to be too much for a sensitive stomach. Scarlett began to get sick, but had nothing to purge except for water. There was not a hint of food dripping from the side of our seat after I helped her sit up.

Weakly, she apologized as she leaned back into my chest, eyes still closed.

So worried about her future for so many reasons, I told her, "It's fine. No need to be sorry."

Tiredly, she moaned, "I want my son."

I grabbed an extra jacket I saw on the seat next to me and laid it over her. "I know. Get some rest now."

Her long sigh at the coverage was full of relief. "That feels *so* warm. Just like you." Her weight sunk into me. "So long since I have been warm, Angel."

Scarlett must have been exhausted from the ordeal. Her breathing changed within seconds, and she fell fast asleep.

Holding the Giordano treasure, there were so many calls I wanted to make. The first one to her mother; Isabella. But, that wasn't possible. The house we had just stolen Scarlett from wasn't the only house that carried danger for her.

That's why, even though we wanted to, we couldn't take her back to our home country yet. We had to hide away this Giordano royalty until it was safe.

In a small town in Idaho, Sal and I—and Mr. Giordano's money—rented a grand, four-bedroom, pristine house on the side of the mountain with incredible views. It was a fair distance from town—best for someone who was overwhelmed by almost everything she laid her eyes upon or heard.

As of that morning, refrigerators were being fully stocked. Now that we had Scarlett, those same extra services would soon be getting clothing for her.

By the time we arrived, it was dark and the temperature was falling. Lights were on inside the house, offering warmth and a beautiful home to slowly expose the world to Scarlett.

Opening the rear passenger door, Sal offered to carry sleeping Scarlett. I still didn't want to release her, but my legs had fallen asleep and I needed to stretch them.

Of course, she woke with alarm, not understanding where or who she was with. Sal assured her, "I will bring you no harm," but she insisted on being put down.

As soon as her bare feet touched the ground, she struggled with the little rocks as if they were strange to the bottom of her soles. Wobbling, and lifting one leg as if not sure what to do, Sal offered her a hand. She was most hesitant but so unstable, she finally accepted, quietly explaining, "The ground... I think it hurts my feet."

"May I pick you up?" Sal's one hand dwarfed both her tied ones as she nervously peered around until seeing me walking toward her.

With stiff shoulders, her eyes filled with tears. "I don't know the right answers."

I picked up the jacket that had fallen to the ground and rested it over her frightened shoulders. "Do you know what instincts are?"

Her stare shot to a sound in the surrounding woods, but she finally nodded. "Belly feelings that Mother said I should follow."

"That's absolutely correct." I gestured to Sal, who was still holding her hands. "Does your belly say he is bad?"

Scarlett, still balancing on one foot, eyed him. A moment later, she shook her head in frustration. "I don't know what is bad or good, but I know what hurts."

I fought the cringe crawling up my spine. "Do you believe Sal will hurt you?"

After another tense pause, she cried out, "I don't know!" while switching her wobbly feet to give one a break on the uncomfortable stones.

Working hard to stay calm, I asked, "Scarlett, may I carry you again?"

Utterly overwhelmed, she nodded while bursting into tears. "I hurt," she banged on her chest, "but no one is hurting me!"

I scooped her up, "That is your heart hurting, sweet woman. That is a pain deep inside," and carried her inside.

It was soul-damaging to remove her ropes for the first time. Where she hadn't scarred over on her wrists, the skin had fused with the rope. She whimpered after Sal and I soaked her skin for the easiest removal possible. There was no way to involve a doctor. This woman technically didn't exist, paperwork-wise. If anyone learned of her, getting her back to Italy would be impossible.

Once she was bandaged up, we offered her food, but she refused. She only wanted a plastic cup of water.

Standing in her bedroom, Sal and I watched her. She looked so uncomfortable sitting in her plush bed, wearing one of Sal's undershirts that drowned her. Her haunted eyes scanned the room as if everything were alive and deadly. Then she found something she recognized.

Without a word, she laid down and stared at her plastic cup that sat on the nightstand. For some reason, this cup was so valuable to her. I think she was afraid when she woke it would be gone, and everything she could comprehend would be gone, too.

How could something so simple be so significant? Her life must have been like nothing I can truly imagine.

Noticing I was struggling to swallow, Sal casually said to me, "Hey, Angel, how about we both sit in these chairs and watch over Scarlett's cup while she sleeps?"

Her eyes lit up as she waited for my answer.

Sucking on my lips, begging myself to force out an answer, I finally choked out, "Sure," and sat down in a chair facing her.

"Perfect!" Sal turned off the lamp. "Try to sleep, Scarlett." He sat in a chair in a corner.

The moonlight was all I needed to watch her. Staring at Scarlett's face, the fact the men called her Scar was perfectly clear. This young woman's beauty was so exquisite she could ruin any man from all other females walking the earth.

Relief filled my chest when her eyes eventually drifted shut.

Throughout the night, Sal and I would wake in our chairs to Scarlett struggling in her sleep. Sal covered his gaping mouth when we watched all her scared movements with her wrists together as if they were still tied.

I promised myself, *I will murder each of those men, slowly.*

In the morning, Sal and I woke, startled when noticing Scarlett was missing. On our feet, running for the door, we both jolted to a stop when finding her sleeping on the floor, in a corner, her plastic cup clutched to her chest.

I walked to the window, rubbing the back of my neck, begging God for guidance.

Thankfully, he gave it to me.

CHAPTER FIVE

Patience. Patience is what it took to be a part of my life. And my Angel had it… May have only had it for me, but he was exactly what I needed. A disciplined man who gave me all the time I required. There were so many hurdles in the beginning.

First one? My son.

It was easy to convince me he wasn't in physical danger after what he had done to me and what I saw he had done to that beautiful grey-eyed young woman. Sal and Angel begged me to become stronger so that, if my son could be saved, I would be able to take care of him. They explained that they believed Seth would need a lot of counseling. They begged me to trust them.

I did. Not because I had no choice, but because of their sincerity. My instincts told me to let them lead the way, for now. There were so many introductions I needed with each and every aspect of a world I was clueless about.

Every bit of growth brought happy, sad, or hostile tears. There was an abundance of emotion inside me, desperately searching for a way to escape. And every tear was needed for me to learn how to move on.

Even things as simple as clothes. I hadn't had any in so many years, so material against my skin felt absolutely foreign.

Rain? It was monumental. I hadn't touched a drop in twenty years. Imagine that. Something so simple, yet so precious, as water falling from the sky. Finally being mine to enjoy again.

The wonders of a 'kitchen' were both mindboggling and fascinating. So many foods now touching my tongue—once I was able to eat more than bland foods, such as broth.

Television?

Sal and Angel chuckled the first time they turned one on and I got up to touch the huge TV mounted on the wall. I had to! My brain couldn't fathom what I was seeing.

When I found a bookshelf, I was mesmerized… Then angry that there were so many words I didn't know.

Sal was so kind. "Would you like me to read to you?"

Mama…

As if I were a child again, I nodded, fighting tears and memories.

Sal grabbed one off the shelf. "Oh, this looks good." He walked back toward the living room. It was so big it outsized the whole house I grew up in. That made it overwhelming as I had mainly been confined to one barren room.

After he sat on the couch, propping up his feet, he was shocked when I crawled into his lap. "Uh, okay."

So ready for this treat, I opened the book he was holding, and then I laid back against his chest and burrowed in. When he didn't start reading right away, I tapped the first page, stumped that he didn't know the routine.

"Uh, yeah." He peered over his shoulder and mumbled, "*This* is going to fly like a lead balloon." He then began to read the book.

A few pages in, Angel walked into the living room. He jolted to a stop.

I waved. "A book!" And pointed. "Sal is reading it to me!"

My nose scrunched as I tried to imitate Angel's flaring nostrils.

Sal asked Angel, "Who was I to say no?"

Italian mumbles echoed as Angel walked out to the back porch, with a view from where we were suspended high in the mountains. Feeling drawn, I was like a moth to the moon, leaving Sal's lap behind to see such beauty. Through a glass door, I walked to Angel's side. He stood at the railing, staring at what I wanted to touch. I even reached out my hand. "I have never seen a mountain up close before."

Angel didn't say anything.

"Have you?" I asked.

His deep voice made my chest tingle. "Yes." He sighed. Maybe because he found it hard to stay angry with me. "Yes, I have. Different countries. Different mountains."

"Maybe I will get to see them with you someday."

"You will see Italy's soon enough."

Movies, TV shows, and the news became another way for me to learn about the world, without being placed in danger from any of them. Distanced, I learned just how detailed and complex the world was.

Angel and Sal had fallen asleep during our movie 'binge' late at night. Neither of them were awake to change the channel—as they often did, for reasons unbeknownst to me back then—when a 'love' scene unfolded. To most moviegoers, it was a beautiful moment between two characters in love. To me, it was horror in its purest form. It was the truth of what I had never known. It was the ultimate example of how all the sex I'd ever had was possibly all wrong. I found myself bitter and longing for something I was confident I had missed out on.

Two captain chairs slowly came to their upright positions when Sal and Angel woke to me standing in front of the flat screen, crying in disbelief and anguish.

Epic confusion, laced with a building torment, almost corrupted all the growth I had experienced so far.

Sal attempted to lay a hand on my shoulder, but I pulled away, pointing at the screen. I fought the growing resentment in my voice. "Why do her tears look happy when that man has sex with her body?"

These two men, in our luxurious hideaway, were not ravishing a woman—me—because they were rich, as it may have appeared to the realtor and maid we had. Sal and Angel were trying to glue together pieces of the broken girl I was, in an attempt to make her whole. They were gently teaching me things, such as the difference between happy and sad tears. They were trying to give me tools to cope with from all I had to heal.

Pointing to the TV, I groaned, yanking on my nightshirt, "*Why* is that *man* not hitting her?"

Angel and Sal just stood there, staring at me, so many thoughts passing through sympathetic eyes that I didn't want.

Deep down—from the darkness trapped inside me—I screamed, "*Where is her rope? Tell me!*" I didn't give them time to explain, nor do I think they could. I just screamed! "*Why is she not tied up?*"

Since the first night I had found the picturesque back porch, that is where you could always find me after I became upset. That's why I ran to the sanctuary of the cold night air, hoping it could cleanse lungs that felt as if they were exploding.

After all I had been through, affection was not an obstacle for the two men when it came to me. My mother had instilled that in me at such a young age. Therefore, I happily accepted it back into my life. That's why, as soon as I felt his heat approach from behind, I turned and melted into Angel's chest, crying. "He was so gentle with her. Why, Angel. Why?"

It took a moment for his arms to wrap around me, but Angel finally held me close to him. His embrace tightened as I cried, begging for answers that were cruel and inhumane. Angel even started swaying his body, soothing mine.

Starting to calm, yet quietly crying, I asked, "Is that how it's supposed to be?"

His answer was so full of regret, I actually felt sorry for him. "Yes." He was the one that had to be brave while confirming my whole life had been one tragic event after another.

Peering up at him, I admitted, "I have never seen or felt that. I want to know what it is like."

After an excuse I could barely hear due to my feelings being in such shambles, Angel left me standing on the beautiful back porch, alone.

When I woke the next day, he was gone.

Sal promised, over and over, that everything was okay—that Angel had errands to run, but loneliness took root. It was the first day since my rescue that I had been without him. Or at least without him in yelling or crying distance.

That evening, Sal was desperate to distract my constant worry, so he asked, "Want to help me cook?" I eyed the hot stove that had recently become an enemy of mine. Probably remembering the incident, Sal laughed. "How about with the salad?"

My stomach grumbling was my answer, but I asked, "Will you teach me how to make that dressing with olives?"

Pleased he successfully had me thinking of something other than Angel, he beamed. "You will make a fine Italian wife someday with the way you love food." He mumbled, "And your tirades."

"Tirades?"

He winked. "You have a true Italian woman's temper."

"Is that bad?"

He huffed. "Hell, no. It is tradition!"

My eyes popped wide. "That sounds wonderful!"

His dress shoes clicked on the sparkly floor as he went to grab a bottle of wine from a cupboard. "It is! The Italian women who raised me *demanded* they be heard." Walking back to the counter, his dark grey slacks moved around what looked to be strong thighs. He grabbed the wine opener while proudly stating, "Your heritage is deep within you, Scar. Someday you will set her free."

Watching him open the bottle of wine, I asked, "Why do you drink that?"

His eyes practically rolled to the back of his head. "You think food tastes good now? Wash it down with a good red and experience your first tastebud orgasm."

"Orgasm?"

"Yeah. When a part of you explodes from something that *feels* or *tastes* so good."

Fascinated, my mouth fell open. "More. Tell me more, Sal."

He gestured to the TV in the open living room part of the kitchen. "Last night. What you saw? That was an orgasm of the heart."

"W-What?" I was starved for such knowledge, dying to experience things that sounded magical to me. "Explain!"

He laughed, but it soon faded... "What your," he did something with his fingers in the air when he said, "fathers—" so I interrupted him.

Mimicking his fingers, I asked, "What does this mean?"

"Uh. Quote. Unquote. It's a way of me showing that I do not agree with what you call those men."

"What *should* I call them?"

"Pieces of shit?"

I thought of the toilet, completely missing his meaning.

Sal must have read my mind because he shook his head. "Not literally. What I mean is... *Fathers* are supposed to nurture daughters. Take care of them. Not hurt them and make them suffer. And fathers should *never* have sex with their children. Never."

Experiencing slight embarrassment due to what Sal had just taught me, I ran my finger along the kitchen counter while head-gesturing to the TV. "That wasn't her father?"

He held his chest then sighed. "No, baby. That was a lover."

It was hard to look Sal in the eye because shame was starting to fill my conscience. "A lover?"

"That's right. Someone you make *love* to. He's not a blood relation. No family. You can *create* a family, have children together, —"

Seth...

"—but... Scar, *your* 'father' mistreated you. He... Well, he had violent sex with you. What he did with, or to, you wasn't love-making. Your body is actually meant to enjoy sex."

My head jerked back. "*Enjoy* it? But it is awful!"

"And there lies the problem. It's not supposed to be awful." A sly smirk crossed his handsome mouth. "Far from it. It can make you feel like, like…" he pondered for an explanation I would comprehend. Then his eyes lit up. "Like you are flying without a plane."

I grabbed my chest. "No."

"Ooh, yes."

"Like a bird?"

"Well," his head wobbled, "figuratively speaking." He started sipping his wine again.

"Wow." This was beyond amazing, and I wanted to know it first-hand! "Sal! You must have sex with me!"

Wine sprayed from his mouth. "Oh." He wiped his chin. "Uh… No."

"What?" My shoulders caved. "You don't want to fly with me?"

He mumbled some Italian, while his finger did a dance at four different points on his chest, then explained, "Your wings have, uh, been *claimed*."

"What does this mean?"

"As gorgeous as you are—" He moaned the next part, "And I have been *months* without some er, '*airtime*', but you will have to *fly* with another."

I rushed to him, placing my palms on his super soft button-down shirt. "Please. I want those happy tears."

"Scar, it just can't be. Not even a taste."

"Please? One little taste?"

Sal sucked in his breath as he stared down at me and winced. "But he is deadly."

"Who?"

He exhaled heavily, then frustratingly mumbled, "Impossible situations. Why won't he just tell you?"

"Who? Angel?"

"Yes."

"What should he tell me?"

"It is not my place to say."

"Fine. Back to the taste." I gripped his shirt and yanked. "Give me one."

He swatted at my hands. "Easy on the silk!"

"Taste!"

"No."

"Please?"

He stared at me.

I asked, "Do other girls like to fly with you?"

"Pfft! Of course. I am *Sal Rossi*." He said his name as if singing a song that he highly admired.

I wanted to admire, too. "Then, you must give me a taste."

He stared at me.

"Sal! You are not my father!"

"No. That I am not."

"Then one little taste. No more. Promise."

Still up against his stomach and chest, I watched as Sal nervously picked up his wine glass, finishing it all in a few big gulps. "For the record, this is a *very* bad idea."

Not sure what he meant, I refused to care. My bare feet ran in place on the cool floor. "Thank you! Thank you! What do I need to do?"

He mumbled something that sounded like, "Not-get-me-killed?"

"What?"

"Nothing." He tilted my chin up. "Hold still, okay?"

I would have never moved again if it would help convince Sal to offer me a piece of magic I had never known.

Golden brown eyes stared at my mouth as Sal slowly lowered his head to reach me. I didn't move an inch. Not even when soft lips pressed to mine.

The sensation was like nothing I had ever felt. It was so… personal. So intimate.

My first taste!

As he pulled his head back, I smiled and said, "Wine. Is that what it tastes like?"

"Wait… Huh?"

I licked my lips. "It is bitter yet… sweet."

"Uh. I just *kissed* you, and you are now curious about wine?"

"Yes." I shrugged. "Is that wrong?"

His brows pinched. "No, I suppose not, but unlike any response I've ever had before."

"I don't understand."

"Well… I'm *Sal*." He said his name as if that should explain everything I needed to know, but I was still confused. When I only stared at him, he shook his head. "Let me try again." This time, he held the sides of my face, like Angel would, and pressed his lips to mine, even harder.

After a lingering moment, he leaned back with a proud smile. "*Now* tell me all you want is *wine*."

"All I want is wine."

Sal gasped, stumbling back as if I had shoved him, then almost cried as he asked himself, "Has *Sal* lost his golden touch?"

Baffled by his comical alarm, I responded, "Gold is very pretty," and poured wine into his glass. "Sal's necklace is beautiful."

I lifted the glass to my lips, but stopped when Sal laid his palm on my forehead. "Maybe you have a fever."

Ignoring him, and ready for my next lesson, I tilted the glass… My mouth *exploded* with taste. "Oh…" I licked my lips. "Wow." I took another sip. "Sal, now *this* is amazing!"

Appalled, he shrieked, "Not my kiss?"

"Can you teach me how to make the dressing now?"

He snatched the glass from me and filled it to the rim. "After I'm done crying away my shame."

By the time Angel finally returned, I was—according to Sal—lounging on the kitchen counter. Sitting on top of a tablecloth, Sal had set me up with my very own glass of wine because he was tired of 'sharing,' slices of cheese, grapes, fresh bread, and olive dressing to dip my bread in. "Angel!" I celebrated. "Would you like to join my pic-i-nic?"

Even though I could tell he was fighting it, Angel smiled. "Pic-i-nic?"

Pulling lasagna from the oven, Sal chuckled. "I told her about all the picnics she will love back home, and how we spend much time next to the orchards with Ma-*Ma*'s cooking. Scarlett wanted an example." He wafted the smell of his lasagna to his nose, using his large hand. Then he moaned in pleasure. Facing Angel again, he explained, "Seeing how we are hanging on the side of the mountain, with no backyard, I improvised." He winked at me. "Who am I to tell her bare feet on the kitchen counter is frowned upon?"

Angel grabbed one of my feet and squeezed, still smiling. "You can do whatever you want."

I gasped. "Can I taste you like I tasted Sal?"

During much arguing in Italian, by Sal and Angel, I waited in my bedroom. Once they finally stopped, and it sounded like they had gone to bed, I snuck out. I was desperate for my plastic cup that Sal had in the 'dishwasher.' Creeping down the hallway, I heard a sound I had never heard. The curious child in me passed by the kitchen and had me following the beautiful noise.

On the other end of the huge living room with the glass walls facing the serene mountains, Angel was sitting on a little stool in front of a black shiny grand piano, his hands moving up and down the keyboard, face focused. With soft lighting, I watched his body move to the music he was creating. He was alluring and intoxicating. My feet carried me to the sight and sounds like a drug calling to an addict.

Angel didn't notice me right away, but when he did and saw what I was wearing, he stopped playing.

Quietly, I pled, "Please don't stop."

"Please stop wearing his undershirt."

Without delay and in one swipe, I removed Sal's shirt, which had become my nightie, and dropped it to the floor. Naked, I demanded, "Play."

Angel's mouth gaped, but his hands found the keys and began to move. So did I. Toward the beautiful sound. I laid my hands on the black wood, yearning for the vibrations. When my bare belly touched the side and felt the music, my whole body bloomed with envy. I wanted to feel the magic all over, in my cells, like I was feeling it in my spirit. Maybe it was the wine, but I had no restraint. I slowly climbed on top of the piano and laid on my back, basking in the beautiful sound and feelings they brought out in me.

As Angel kept playing the lovely melody, my eyes slid shut, and I surrendered to the utopia happening inside me. My arms lifted over my head to reach for the maestro soothing my soul. When his face leaned into my hands, I felt high because of the music rushing through me while I touched its creator.

I thought of Sal and how he told me about body orgasms, and I was sure I was having one. It felt that uplifting—like soaring through valleys I'd never seen. And for once, I was carrying no fear, for I had my angel to guide the way.

He kept playing as I rolled over, needing to see the one strumming the chords in my heart. "Angel." I pulled my body forward until my face was close to his. "Please." I opened my eyes that felt lazy, happily so. "Let me taste you." I cupped the face that brought me solace. "It would mean so much to me."

As if entranced, Angel leaned forward, his hands playing the piano by touch alone, and pressed strong lips to mine.

Suddenly, the piano no longer had my full attention. It belonged to the man that made me instantly ache. He didn't taste like wine. He didn't taste like anything I had ever experienced. But I now knew it was all I would ever want.

My eyes slid shut, just like the first time I had tasted chocolate ice cream. I wanted to dive into the bowl Sal had filled, wanted to have more. I couldn't even stop licking the spoon because of the mind-blowing flavor caressing my tongue.

But, after such a kiss, I was positive Angel would be even more desirable. "Angel, lick me."

A melody caressed my belly through the piano, and as Angel's lips opened, they caressed my soul. His soft, wet tongue licked at my lips before sliding into my mouth. My whole body burst in celebration, causing me to moan inside his mouth.

I wasn't sure what spurred this man to react, but his lips got hungrier and his tongue deeper, the piano louder. Our breaths battled, as did our lips…

Then, without warning, the song drifted to an end, right after his mouth slowly pulled away from mine.

Eyes still closed, my head fell forward. I had just flown. Angel set me on a flight I would treasure, always. "You are my wings, Angel."

When he didn't reply or kiss me again, my eyes drifted open, only to see… he was gone.

Sitting on a bench swing on the back porch, I held my plastic cup of water and watched the sunrise. Sal came outside and, after laying a blanket over my naked body, sat next to me.

He complained, "I hate that you are so accustomed to the cold."

I leaned into him, happy he had placed his arm around my shoulders. "Being able to adapt is better than suffering, right?"

He kissed the top of my head. "Such a fast learner."

After a moment more of the same thoughts that had kept me up all night, I asked, "Sal, why would Angel not want me to wear your shirt?"

He chuckled. "As I said, your 'wings' have been claimed."

"Meaning?"

"He doesn't want to share you."

I leaned my head against his shoulder. "Being shared is all I've ever known."

"Well, Angelo is different. He cares for you. Deeply."

"Then why did he leave me twice yesterday?"

Sal blew out air and let his head fall back against the swing. "Truth?"

"Why would I want a lie?"

He chuckled again, lifting his head to watch the sunrise. "Good question." His hand squeezed my shoulder before he told me, "You are a *Giordano*. Your mother's blood makes you very special in my and Angel's world—our line of work. We are not of your bloodline."

Not my bloodline… He could be a lover!

Sal continued, "Neither of us would ever be permitted to ever be, uh… *with* you."

"With me?"

"A boyfriend or husband prospect."

Prospect… For some reason, that word triggered a response in me. And a flashback. *"Fuck her good, Prospect—"*

"What's wrong?" asked Sal.

I blinked, my chest tightening. "I'm, uh, not sure."

My mind suddenly heard loud noises… "Engines."

"Like the car?"

My eyes slammed shut as I felt many hands on me. *"Harder Prospect!"*—

"Angel!" yelled Sal.

My mouth tried to word… "Pro… spect."

"What happened?" yelled Angel, his shoes pounding onto the back porch.

Sal sounded so worried. "I-I don't know!"

I was sucked back into the memory… *"Move, you worthless shit!" Different hands grabbed me. "Like this!"*— I screamed out in pain!

"Scarlett!"

When my eyes opened, I was now standing, my hands over my head as if I were tied again, my heart pounding. Gasping for air, I numbly peered down when I heard my plastic cup rolling across the outside tile.

Angel was in front of me. "Can you see me?"

Leather vests… "Angel?"

"Right here." He reached up and held my hands, even though the restraint was only in my imagination—memory, putting us so close, I instantly felt some ease. "Right in front of you."

But then my mind snapped back to the memory. *Vrooooom. Vrooooom…* My eyes snapped shut, wanting the flashbacks to end, yet needing to express what I was seeing. "T-Two tired cars."

"Two tired—W-What?" Angel aggressively cupped my face, then sternly demanded, "Scarlett, look at me."

As my arms came down, I felt faint. "Scar. My name is Scar."

More memories haunted me. *"Scar, I'm gonna fuck you until you—"* My legs felt weak. "The Prospect."

Angel pulled me to him. "Shh. No more prospects." The way he said it was as if he understood more of what I was saying than I did. "You're safe now. No one will touch you again." Then, he growled Italian words to Sal. The only ones I could understand were *steel stallions*.

Sal, sounding just as angry, tapped on his phone while adding to the conversation in Italian.

Between strained breaths, I said, "Please don't shut me out of conversations."

Angel guided me back to the swing and sat me down, tucking me into his side. "I'm sorry. We just didn't want to alarm you, but we are now understanding more of your past."

Sal squatted in front of me, his hands holding my knees. "Scar, I think you have hidden memories."

"Is that possible?"

He ran fingers through his lighter hair. "Yes, unfortunately."

My lungs started to seize again. "I wish I had a different life."

Angel's warm arms tightened around me. "Shh. Focus on something else until it is easier for you to breathe."

Sal quietly said, "I will fill her cup," and walked away.

"Easier to breathe?" I asked Angel. "Like what?" I sniffled.

"Something that has made you happy."

That was easy. I had very few times to choose from. And most were all recent. I let my mind wander to Angel playing the piano and… *our kiss*. Quickly, I found myself melting to his side.

He was pleased. "That's better. Whatever you are thinking about, keep doing so."

Even though I was so upset, this memory actually brought me so much happiness, I smiled. "I will never forget it."

Sal returned with my water and asked, "What won't you forget?"

I sighed. "What Angel tasted like."

"Is that so?" Lifting a brow, Sal delivered a sinister smile to Angel. "Anything you wish to share?"

My head tilted. "I thought Angel doesn't want to share me."

Angel's jaw dropped, right before he returned a glare to Sal.

That evening, in the living room, Angel tried to explain that, because of my family in Italy, my marriage would be arranged to prosper my grandfather's legacy. Yes, a man whose poor decisions had my mother kidnapped and me born into slavery, now had control over the biggest decisions of *my* life.

"No," I growled.

"But," argued Angel, "it is how it is done."

"Then I'm not going to Italy."

"Scarlett, be reasonable," pled Angel.

"Stop calling me that! I am Scar!"

"But Scar is a name *they* called you."

"It is all I've known for twenty years!"

He raised his hands, something he did often to calm me. "Okay. Okay… That name may be something familiar to you, but it reminds me of what I saw the day we found you. Is it possible we compromise?"

I snarled, "I don't even know what that means!"

Now it was Sal, behind the kitchen island, silently gesturing for me to breathe and calm myself right before he poured cooked noodles into a strainer. He knew how much I loved his homemade alfredo.

Angel said, "If you stay calm, I will explain." He waited until I agreed to listen. "Okay. Thank you. A compromise is like a trade. A way to 'meet in the middle'." He took a step toward me and waited.

Frustrated, but too curious to not be willing to learn, I took a step toward him.

When his hands cupped my face, I instantly settled, sighing at the sensation. His touch was like a whisper of the heavens he swore he did not come from.

Angel stared deep… "The very first time I saw these magnificent eyes, they reminded me of the galaxy where the stars hang in the sky. Endless and mesmerizing. I still see you this way, a limitless being who is learning her freedom."

His presence and words made my heart race. "Angel—"

His thumb caressed my lips. "I don't belong to heaven, but will fight to belong to a star."

Rhymes from the stories my mother had read me caught in my breath. Angel was trying to tell me something. *Scar… Star…* A compromise.

I swallowed. "That is… a good trade."

His brutally serious face always softened when I made him smile.

We stood there, staring at each other.

His stomach began to move as he fought for his breath.

It was happening to me, too. "You want to taste me again?" I was full of pure joy.

Angel, hungrier than I'd ever witnessed him, had us face to face in the blink of an eye. Italian words danced across my face as he whispered them.

"W-What did you just say?"

His eyes closed as if he were fighting for control. "Nothing."

From the kitchen, Sal piped in, "He said he wants to ravage you." Angel quickly glared over his shoulder in warning, but Sal only shrugged. "Hey, don't look at me like that. I only make her want to drink wine. Speaking of," he glanced about, "where is my glass?"

Hopeful, I asked Angel, "Is *ravage* good?"

He released me. "No." And turned away.

Sal fake-coughed. "Liar."

Why would Angel lie to me?

Fighting emotions that brought even more confusion to my damaged heart, I asked, "Why? Why won't you touch me like that?"

Walking away from me, Angel grumbled, "Like what?"

"The movie."

"Because you do not know what you are asking of me."

A wicked laugh escaped my now raging soul. "I am very aware of what being fucked by a man feels like."

That made Angel angry. He was back in my space. "See? You *don't* know. I wouldn't *fuck* you. I would *worship* you."

From around Angel's thick bicep, I peeked at Sal to silently ask if being worshipped was a good thing. Drinking his wine, he gave me a thumbs up.

That was all I needed to know. I lifted my chin to Angel. "Then worship me."

"No." Angel turned away from me again.

"Why not?"

"I already explained. You will be someone else's."

"*I* already explained to *you* that I have *not* been taken from one captivity only to be placed in another!"

He turned and pointed at me. "You will go where I tell you to go."

"*Angelo*," warned Sal.

Angel faced him and yelled something in Italian. In response, Sal's hand was waving through the air as he yelled back.

As beautiful as the language was to me, I still became angry from being locked out of the conversation, yet again. I had learned a few words but could not keep up with them both so angry and speaking impossibly fast. "Speak English!"

Sal dipped his chin to me while saying, "*Angelo*, she does not see you as merely someone to have sex with."

Angel's back to me made it impossible to miss his shoulders cringing.

That made my chest feel sharp pains. The sharp pains made me furious. Immediately.

At the time, I didn't comprehend how I related pain to being trapped, but that was my poison. I rushed to the piano and slammed my hands down on the ivory keys. "Here! You kissed me here!"

"Yes!" cheered a pleased Sal, wine glass high in the air. "Yes, *Italian* woman! Show me your fight!"

Every chance that man had, he always reminded me I had roots beyond the captivity I associated with everything.

I slammed my hands down again, the piano crying out for mercy. "I am not broken!"

Sal bellowed out more Italian words that sounded to be full of pride and answered prayers.

Angel, out of breath, rushed to me. "I believe you. I do. But you have been through so much. Your past—"

"Then give me something worth holding on to in my future."

"I—" His eyes slammed shut. "I can't."

"You can!" I grabbed his head and forced him to kiss me.

"Claim your man!" cheered Sal.

Angel pulled his lips from mine. Placing our foreheads together, he softly spoke, "Your grandfather—"

"Is nothing to me."

"Is your family."

Knowing I was gaining ground with Angel, I decided to take advantage. "Okay. Then let us compromise."

A grand smile crossed Angel's lips as laughter echoed from the kitchen. Sal, so pleased, stated, "*Damn*, she learns quick."

Angel beamed, so proud of me. "Okay, *Star*, what is the trade?"

I took a deep breath… "I'll go back to Italy if you help me fly."

With his brows furrowed together, Sal fake-coughed again, "She means sex."

"Oh." Releasing me, Angel stepped back.

I grabbed his hands, so strong I felt his essence through my whole body. "Please let me feel those happy tears."

He shook his head. "Star, there is no guarantee you will like it. Plus, how could I ask you to want another male body after what they did to you? How could you even trust me in a bed?"

Pulling his hands to my face, I pleaded, "How can you not trust me to know what I need or want?" That made his spine stiffen, so I nodded. "Yes, you keep telling me to think for myself, but when I do, you tell me I am wrong." He hissed, trying to lean away from me, but I held on. Through a desperate whisper, I promised, "I trust you."

After a long moment, he respectfully spoke, "What an honor to hear such words from you. Thank you. But if I did anything wrong, in a bedroom, to you—Not that I would ever hurt you, but what if, mentally, something I do triggers you? What if I cause more harm than good?" Not pulling from my hands holding him to my cheeks, his thumbs ran across my skin. "That would cause me more pain than you can understand."

"Ah, shit," mumbled Sal from the kitchen.

Angel peered over his shoulder. "You understand me now?"

Sal's head hung forward, his hands bracing on the kitchen counter. "Yeah, I understand now. I hadn't thought of that."

And there was my no. No wings for Star. Forever will she be scarred.

My bottom lip trembled, but I kept my head high. "I would never want you in pain."

Adoration poured from him to me.

We stood there, staring at each other…

Until… "Wait." Sal released a menacing chuckle. "Sal may have a solution." We both looked to Sal, who was smug as he held up a spaghetti noodle, his eyebrows dancing. When neither of us caught his meaning, he flung the noodle at Angel. "*You* be the man without hands."

CHAPTER SIX

The Linked One

There is possibly nothing sexier than a hungry—deadly—mafia—Italian—man, tied to your bed. There is possibly nothing more freeing than not being the one restrained. Every choice, every movement was mine to decide.

Angel's thick chest was bare, but from mid-stomach down, a blanket covered him, so I asked, "Do you know I have seen a naked man before?"

Angel's eyes closed as if not wanting to picture my past. When they reopened, his jaw had locked. "I also know there was no option offered to you."

I raised my hands. "Fair trade." His body relaxed and sank back into the mattress as he watched me slowly approach the bed. "Do your wrists hurt?"

Compassion crossed his face as he sunk deeper into the mattress. "No."

"Angel… I don't know where to start."

His hand jerked to a stop when he tried to reach out for me. As he stared at his restraints, I realized two things. Angel was a man very used to being in control, and he just had an inkling of what it was like to be me. A sad smile crossed his lips. "Start wherever you want."

In a nightie that was not Sal's shirt, I sat on the edge of the bed next to the man that had found his way into a heart that I was clueless how to control. Maybe that was the secret, to not try and tame the roaring love I had to offer. "How do you feel when imagining me marrying a man in Italy?"

Angel's restrained hands made fists. "It doesn't matter."

Softly, I said, "It does," I patted my chest, "to me."

His hands relaxed in surrender, and his voice was barely audible, "It hurts."

My eyes slid shut in relief. "Thank you." My body melted to his side and laid half on top of him. "Thank you." Slowly, I crawled up his body. "Thank you." A leg on each side of his hips, I pressed my lips to his... "Now make me fly."

How a dangerous man could be a perfect and sensitive lover can only be answered by the divine, because that is who he was created by. Now, he was mine to enjoy.

Breathlessly, he told me, "You being so close has me already soaring."

A pure and free smile broke free from me. "Thank you."

Our lips joined for a sensual kiss where I was in charge. I explored his mouth until my stomach ached. "A-Angel." My mouth, though gasping for air, refused to stop touching him. "My belly is... tight."

His broad chest expanded underneath me through his every pant. "That means your wings are stretching. They are getting hungry for air."

My open lips caressed his face before joining with his lips again. When his tongue swiped mine, I moaned, diving deeper to taste more of this stunning man.

I gazed up when I felt his arms go taut. "Angel, are you wanting to be free?"

He hungrily kissed me, "Just my wings stretching, too," then he sucked my bottom lip into his mouth.

I groaned. "Oh yes, please do that again."

As my lip was pulled into his mouth, our breaths fought for space we both refused to offer, so we inhaled one another whole.

"Angel," I rasped out. "The ache. It is moving."

"Let it. Follow it. Become it." He swallowed as if it took much effort. "Your wings are searching for a wind to lift you off the ground."

Nodding, trusting him, my open mouth moved from his face to his neck. "Can I kiss you here?"

Breathing loudly, his head fell to the side. "Of course."

After placing kisses like I had never delivered before, my hungry tongue swiped up his neck to taste my Italian ice-cream.

A deep groan rose from the chest below me, making me want even more. As I slid down his body slightly, I asked, "Can I kiss you here?"

His chest stretched with every labored breath. "Do anything you want to me."

Blindly, I latched onto his nipple.

In a lusty response, Angel arched, then started speaking rapid Italian.

I lapped at his delicious flavor. "Good words, Angel?"

"Yes." His arms fought the dinner napkins Sal had tied him up with. "*Yes.*"

Frustrated with my tightly wound body, I bit the other side of his chest. "Ache. I ache."

His hiss was accompanied by a pelvic thrust. He quickly stopped himself. "Oh, Star, I'm sorry—"

His erection touching my core shot a sensation through my whole body, like striking a match, setting an instant blaze. I growled, "Do it again."

He could barely talk around his loss of air. "Are you sure?"

I bit his chest. Hard.

Angel's hips surged up, lifting me from the bed. As he carried me back down, I lazily sat up, yearning for more friction. My head hung forward. "Angel."

His stomach muscles curled under my hands as his hips obeyed me. "I'm right here with you, *bella donna*."

His voice, his heat, the Italian language… and my body coming to life, all had me swaying. "What does that mean?"

"Beautiful woman."

Everything stopped, and my ears began to ring.

My eyes opened. "Say that again."

His strained face softened as he realized what had touched me most, even more than his magnificent body. "You are *so* beautiful."

My eyes filled with tears. I had never heard kind words during a sexual experience. As tears fell, my lips trembled through a tragic but sincere smile. "You did it, Angel. As my lover, you gave me happy tears."

His mouth fell open as he stared at me, no longer thrusting his hips.

Happier than I had ever been, I whispered, "Thank you."

His smile was… everything. "Star, untie me."

My body raced up his, my legs tangling around his head as my shaky hands fought his restraints. As soon as one was untied, a stout arm wrapped around me, a gentle hand spread against my back.

I leaned into the touch. "I love your hands on me."

His fingers tightened with such strength I felt a wetness pool between my legs. "They never want to let you go."

His words, his meaning, his touch, all of it was euphoric. Drugged. I felt drugged as I bathed in his affection. As soon as his other hand was successfully untied, I melted, now surrendering to the man who had hands.

Easily accepting my weight, Angel sat up and engulfed me in his strong arms. He possessed me, heart and soul. With me straddling his lap, we fell into a kiss that would last me a lifetime. It was even more passionate than our piano kiss. I was lost in him. I was *found* in him.

"Angel—" My head rolled as an exotic sensation barreled through my body, one that had never been permitted to feel anything other than pain. "I don't want clothes between us." He lifted my nightie over my head and threw it. "I don't want sheets between us." His feet and legs kicked the sheet free. I sunk onto his naked, heated skin. "Yes. I want all of you." His erection throbbed underneath me. My insides felt like the waves of water I saw in the children's book my mother would read me. "Angel, show me everything I missed as a young woman." Lips kissed me everywhere he could reach. My neck, my chest, my shoulders… "Do to me what should have been done." My body was lifted and laid on the bed. "Give me every part of you."

Angel laid on top of me, his heavy body sheltering me from all past memories.

I cried out… "I ache."

He lifted and pushed my leg to the side, making room for his wide hips.

"Higher." My wings were taking flight.

I could feel him at my entry as he said, "The best part of flying is learning how to fall."

Angel pushed inside me, causing an explosion that had me arching and thanking every star in the night sky.

My mouth was wide, inhaling beautiful air, then it got to inhale the man who was trying to swallow me whole. Oh, the wonderful sensation of drowning, and flying, and falling, all at the same time. His hips surged and pumped and thrust, taking me to places I had *never* known.

I was overwhelmed and at peace.

I was soaring and crashing.

I was delighted and emotional.

I was fulfilled, and I was drained.

I was with my Angel of Death… who brought me back to life.

I woke to wet heat between my legs. I was naked and on my back, my thighs spread wide. Broad shoulders and a head full of dark hair was what I could see in the dark, but what I felt was Angel's mouth. My core quickly began to thrum. Silently, it begged for him to never stop the delicious attack. Then, a powerful thumb swiped at the most sensitive part of my body that I didn't even know I had.

A needy groan climbed up my throat.

A chuckle vibrated against my channel, right before I felt another swipe.

It almost felt like I was bearing down, holding my breath, as Angel gave that spot more attention with his thumb or tongue.

I begged, "Please, please, please. I-I don't know what you are doing, but please don't stop."

"After tasting you, stopping is never going to happen."

Then his mouth latched on and owned my core. My whole body began to tremble, frantically, to the point I started to become alarmed, but then I went blind.

A scream ripped from my throat as my body exploded into so many colors.

Angel never stopped. He sank fingers inside me and had his mouth torturing me with heaven on his tongue.

When I started convulsing, he finally eased his spell on me.

With my body completely spent, there was no fight in me as he crawled up the bed and pulled my back to his stomach, curling his heated body around mine. My eyes were already drifting shut as he whispered in my ear, "I thought you would like to try another set of wings that you have had hidden."

I think I nodded, but I'm not sure. My body had never been so sated. So jellified. I was so relaxed, I slept deeper than ever before.

By morning, I awoke to a knock at Angel's bedroom door. He pulled a sheet over me as Sal entered—without permission—holding a tray of food, coffee, and orange juice. It smelled so good that my stomach started to rumble. By the time Sal was standing at my side of the bed, my eyes found the strength to drift open.

One look and Sal started laughing! "Wow! I see my man took *very* good care of his Italian woman."

On my side, I couldn't move. Still spent, I just laid there, smiling. "He is better than your chocolate ice-cream."

At my back, a warm chest rumbled.

Sal teased, "But still doesn't taste as good as my wine kiss, right?" He jerked backward as a large arm flew over me and swatted. "Hey! Don't make me spill the coffee on the silk!"

Angel laughed, pulling my lazy body impossibly closer to him. "Put the tray down and get the fuck out."

Sal set it on the nightstand. "Can I at least get a thank you?" He winked at me before walking back around the bed toward the door. "I've been trying to get her to gain weight, and now you're burning more of her calories than I can get into her."

My chest boomed with adoration as I realized the man had been cooking nonstop, not only because he loved food as much as me, but because I was far too skinny to be healthy.

The girl without hands had gone from horrific abuse to an abundance of love.

Maybe fairytales can truly exist.

Three months later...

Staring at the mountains, now full of snow, I was reminded of the cold of the basement, even though I was warm. Why? The answer laid in the impossible. How can you love someone in such a short amount of time? How can you find peace in a stranger whose soul now speaks to yours? That's what it was like to have Angel in my life.

I was petting my tiny little Yorkshire dog, who I had named Bella after my mother, when Angel's stern voice asked, "You are packed and ready, correct?"

I will miss you, mountains. The time had come for me to fly to the country that I would soon call home. "I am."

Angel exhaled. "Please stop being angry with me."

I faced him, shivering but not from the cold. Angel had yet to put his jacket on; therefore, all his gun holsters and weapons were clear to see. "Please let them handle this."

Angel took a step toward me but caught himself. Our mountain getaway was now occupied with deadly Italian Mafia men, all preparing for revenge and... "I need to be there to search for Seth."

My eyes slid shut. *My son.*

"Star," growled Angel, so I opened my eyes. "Meet me in Sal's room."

Frustrated, I nodded, then, when no one was watching, the 'Giordano Princess' slid into the dark room. Bella was taken from me and set on Sal's bed before I was shoved against the wall, a heated and suited man pushing his body to mine. Our lips mashed together with anger toward having to hide in a house where I had learned to be so free, and because we were not allowed to love each other.

"Tell me," he growled, "that you understand."

"It doesn't mean I have to like it."

Lips battled in the dark. Hands gripped and groped.

Knock, knock. Sal snuck in. "Angelo, they are waiting."

Angel aggressively kissed me one more time. "Be ready."

Then he left me in the dark.

Sal handed me back Bella, then kissed my cheek, promising they would both be okay. The room was eerily quiet after he shut the door, following Angel.

I stood there, fighting a shock that wanted to take hold. The two men I adored were off to a gunfight… If they were to live and succeed, we were all to load onto a private jet and race back to Italy.

Thankful the wall was supporting me, I laid a hand on my flat stomach. What I hadn't told Angel was that he would soon be a father.

What if he dies? I covered my mouth to contain my gasp and fear. *He has to know!*

I ran out of the bedroom and into an empty living room. "No."

I ran to the front door and swung it open.

I was too late.

Wheels were spinning, and cars raced from the driveway.

As I watched Angel drive off, I had no idea that he was joining a battle that would link us in ways that could not be undone.

Blood.

Blood, murder, revenge, and family.

How could we ever have known the son I was carrying, our Mafia Prince, would someday fall in love with the princess of the Steel Stallions, creating a *Hostile Grace.*

Thank you so much for reading this book that was incredibly dark. It hurt to write, and most likely hurt to read, but I am grateful for your empathy toward a damaged soul who deserves love and respect. She has quite a journey ahead of her. Thankfully, she has a guardian *angel*, too. ;)

Want more of this story, *The Man With A Treasure* can be yours now!
(Read a sneak peek of the book at the end of this one!)

For those of you who have read *Bleed Me*, the interconnected stand-alone novel in my **Haunted Roads** series, I hope you enjoyed that surprise, and are still breathing. I'm super excited for *Hostile Grace* in my **Steel Stallions MC** series!!

For those of you who would like to try my other series that tie into this one, I have **Haunted Roads, Steel Stallions MC,** and **Redemption Ryders MC**. If you are wondering where a good place to start is, you can try *Steal Me*, or signup for my newsletter and get the five-star novella, *Hostile Illusions* for free!
If you have any questions, feel free to email me, or join my reader group and ask!
Myself, my PA, or my readers would be delighted to show you the India Map ;)

INDIA'S THANK YOUS

Even though *The Girl Without Hands* is a very short story compared to my novels, it still takes a team for me to release a book.

Let the thank yous begin…

Cat, thank you for handling my crazy like a trained pro! I'm pretty sure no one envies your job. I am an artist, through and through, and have the chaotic brain to prove it. Yet, you constantly keep me from falling apart. You are my star in the night and a cherished friend! You Alpha read, make me beautiful artwork covers at TRC Designs, format my books… and you manage to love me, even though I have you going in a thousand directions at once. Your talent is endless. Thank you.

Lindsay, my Uni, Post Master, Boo-Boo Finder, and beautiful friend, thank you for *everything*!

Deb, thank you for being one of the first in my work! Thank you for being everything that you are. Your support, advice, and heart are so special to me. Deep inhale…

Jay, thank you for the Slay Belle Anthology cover!! It is wickedly perfect!!

Kendra, what would I do without my editor? Lose my sh— That's what! Thank you for being so much more than my word fixer. I impatiently wait for the day I get to finally hug you.

Michelle! You have entered my world by a storm I hope never ends. Not only have you been so kind as to speak so highly of my work, but now you are a part of it! Thank you for jumping in when I needed another beta reader. I am grateful.

India Flames, Sparks, Igniters, and Bloggers, you may not be a hot alpha Italian Mafia stud-muffin, but you are most certainly the wind beneath my wings. I love you all!!!

Family, even though we are doing our best to survive a pandemic, personal life tribulations, and challenges that keep popping up because 2020 is from the bowels of Hell, we have become stronger for it, and you *still* stand faithfully, by my side, so I can continue this dream of being a writer. I love you more than words can ever express.

FREE BOOK!

Get this book FREE when you sign up to my newsletter!

Sign up on my website: www.indiaradams.com

BOOKS BY INDIA

The Giordano Mafia

The Girl Without Hands

The Man With A Treasure

The Men With A War (coming soon)

Haunted Roads

Steal Me

Scar Me

Bleed Me

The Haunted Roads Boxset

Steel Stallions MC

Hostile Illusions

Hostile Saint (Coming April 2021)

Redemption Ryders MC

Road to Absolution (Coming Soon)

Tainted Water

Blue Waters

Black Waters

Red Waters

Volatile Waters

Ashen Waters (Coming Soon)

Forever

Serenity

Destiny

Mercy

Hope (Coming Soon)

A Stranger in the Woods

Rain

River

Mist

The Travelers - A standalone (Coming June 11th 2021)

Standalones

My Wolf and Me

Ivy's Poison

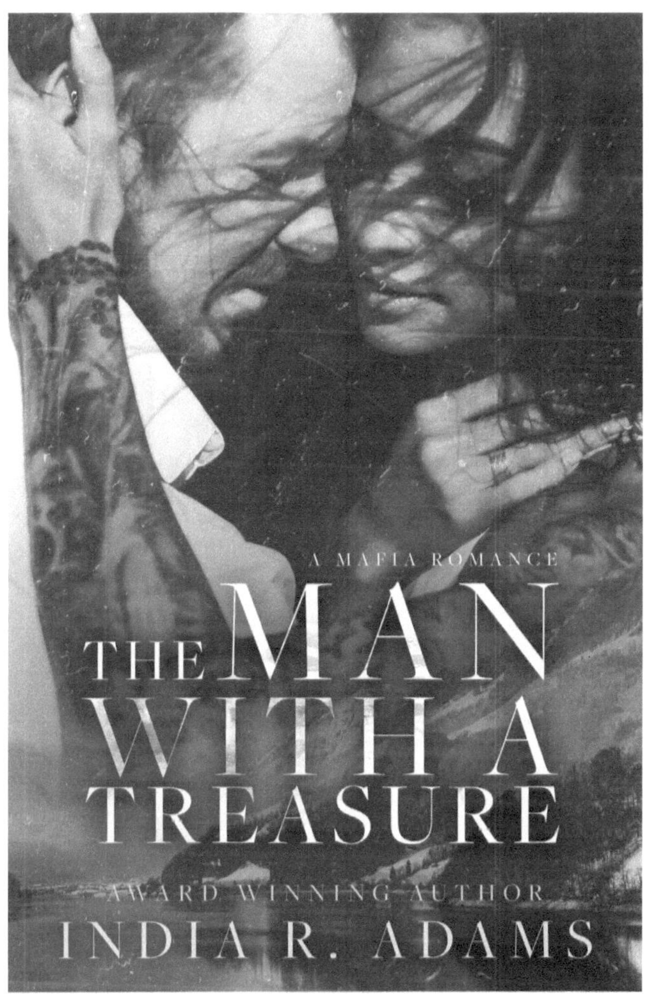

Turn the page for a first look at The Man With a Treasure!

PROLOGUE

The Valiant One

In the cold and barren room, the woman held the child close. The only blanket she had to offer was the warmth of her love. That love flowed through her, just like the story she was whispering, "… His wings, so grand, they almost blocked out the dark sky…"

Gasp! The child was mesmerized by the tale her mother was sharing. On their torn and empty mattress, she whispered, "The Angel of the Night, Mamma?"

The woman wished she could finish the story, but knew time was running out. Not only was the moon shining through their only bedroom window, but the men who held them captive could be heard on the other side of the locked door. The lock was not for her protection. It was for her imprisonment, as were the bars on the window.

The sound of her drunk jailers struggling with the key in the door made her naked body tremble, but she still answered her child, "Yes, it was." The woman's heart pounded as she gently nudged her daughter to face the wall. To hide her fear, she softly said, "It is time to go to sleep, *Vita Mia*. Remember not to open your eyes or you will miss your *dreams*."

The little girl—only about the age of five—faced the wall as she always did when told and closed her eyes. "I hope I dream of the Angel, Mamma."

Seven sets of heavy footfalls echoed in the dark room as she replied, "As do I." Mean hands pulled the woman from the bed and pushed her to the floor, as she cried in silence. "As do I." Her body used to suffering the common abuse, she thought to herself, *May he come and take you away, my Vita Mia.*

CHAPTER ONE

In Italy within the *Giordano* family may have not been the ideal place to raise a teenager, but my father was the head of security, and so that is where I grew up. After my mother died, my twelve-year-old self was delivered to my father, a man I had rarely seen. Up to this point, he had only provided for me monetarily. Now that he was to be my full-time caregiver, I was nervous, hoping the larger-than-life stranger would accept me into his own life. Without my mother or her family, I felt lost.

The Mercedes that had picked me up from my uncle's house looked and smelled more expensive than anything I had ever experienced. My aunt, my mother's sister, cried terribly as they pried me from her loving arms, forcing me to leave behind all that I had known. As a man, I now understand her tears weren't merely because she would miss me. They were also tears borne of fear. She knew the lifestyle in which I was about to be introduced and trained to live.

Italy is beautiful. Where I was headed was no different, just much more rural. There were no other houses, just hills off in the distance. Eventually, we pulled down a dirt and gravel road that felt endless. I stared at the rows and rows of grapevines. There was nothing else to do since the car's driver hadn't spoken a word to me over the last hour.

Finally reaching a clearing, I saw sizeable trees with canopies sheltering conjoined wooden tables, enough for large gatherings, all standing in front of a house that resembled a castle. Guarding the castle were several men in black suits, one of whom had a rifle casually resting in his arms. They all wore dark sunglasses and were watching our car approach.

As we parked, dust from the dirty road settled and the impressive front door opened. Exiting was the man I had seen at Christmas when his arms had been full of gifts. He walked toward me as I got out of the car. My eyes looked to the ground in a nervous manner.

"Eyes up," in Italian, barked the man who had spawned me. *"Always know your surroundings."*

His dominance had me doing exactly as he demanded. *"Yes, sir."* I studied above me to avoid his heavy stare. There were strings of lights in the tree, making me curious as to what they looked like at night. My mother could never afford such things. I startled when noticing a boy my age staring down at me with golden brown eyes and lighter hair. I pointed up. *"I am being watched."*

My father, now standing in front of me, dipped his chin. *"Well done."* He peered up. *"Come down and meet my son."*

The boy dropped from the tree and stood next to us. With a huge smile, he shared, *"Hello, I am Sal."* He leaned back and proudly opened his arms. *"Sal Rossi."*

Even at the tender age of twelve, Sal had swagger and impressive self-esteem.

Not quite so confident, I replied, *"Hello, I am Angelo."* I looked to my father, not feeling nearly as proud as Sal of the name I carried. *"Bianchi."*

Sal kept smiling. *"Welcome, Dark Angel, finding his roots."* He spoke with a 'knowing' expected from an elder in a family. Since he was so young, I felt his claim to be wrong until I looked at my attire—which was what he was apparently judging.

I winced, seeing he was right. I was dressed in a black T-shirt, black jeans… It was late spring. I should have been in lighter colors to avoid the sun baking me while working in my uncle's fields. Now, peering at my father in a dark suit, it was hard to deny my subconscious may have been trying to imitate the parent I had, apparently, been longing for.

Instantly, a little guilt pelted my heart. Would my mother be disappointed in me since she did not have many kind words to share about the man who had destroyed her future? According to her, their marriage had not been of love, but of responsibility, because he impregnated the young naïve Italian girl. When I was four, my father's priority with the Giordanos outweighed his responsibility to us, and he left my mother and me for good, only to return on a few holidays.

Reminders of my resentment had me daring to ask, "*Father, why am I here? My uncle was willing to provide for me.*"

"*Your loyalty no longer lies with him.*"

That was it. I had been claimed and would now follow my father's footsteps, whether I wished to or not.

Now, all I felt I could offer was gratitude for the one thing he had given me. "*Thank you for allowing me the time to finish mourning.*" Even though I was positive mourning and grieving for my mother would never end.

My father only dipped his chin, not mentioning my mother's name, which was common practice for us superstitious ones.

I gestured to the security guards. "*What is being hidden here?*"

My father lifted a brow. "*Hidden?*" He shook his head. "*No. We are protecting.*"

"*Protecting what?*"

"*What belongs to the Giordanos.*"

What *belongs to* the Giordanos, was complicated yet simple. The simple definition was one dark trade for another. The complicated part was how many innocents would be caught up in the illegal dealings, and how all involved, including myself, would pay.